The gods smile upon a weary warrior...

Brenn, a warrior returning home from battle, rests by a tempting magical pool and meets a siren who changes his life forever.

Bound by a curse, he must find a way to save his pride.

He returns from a war far from his home to find that his village is destroyed and his pride missing. With the help of his guardian dragon, Ciara, he sets out to find his missing family and pride.

After Ciara saves Brenn's life twice, he begins to realize that he is not as invincible as he once thought. He must accept his limitations and the help of his lifemate to keep him safe.

In Search of Pride
Copyright © 2017 Taryn Jameson and Gabriella Bradley
ISBN: 978-1-4874-1643-0
Cover art by Angela Waters

Published by eXtasy BooksInc

Look for us online at:
www.eXtasybooks.com or www.devinedestinies.com

IN SEARCH OF PRIDE
CRIMSON REALM CHRONICLES
BOOK 1

BY

TARYN JAMESON AND GABRIELLA BRADLEY

DEDICATION

Taryn Jameson – *There are two very important women in my life that have influenced me greatly. My mother, who always told me that I could accomplish anything I set out to do, and the woman who has made so many of my dreams possible. This is for you.*

Gabriella Bradley – *To my co-writer, whose tiny 1200 word story inspired this series. It continues to be a fun ride dreaming up fantasies as we complete book 7, Initiation Genesis...*

CARNAL TWILIGHT

THE PREQUEL

Brenn wearily slid off his horse by the silvery pool of water. He knew of the legends and superstitions that surrounded the pool, but after a long day of travel, the gurgling waterfall sang to him of its healing power. The pool was bottomless, housing fearsome creatures, it was said. What had he to fear of the superstitions of peasants? He was a warrior. The gods smiled upon him, showering him with wealth and the spoils of war.

His pride had held many sacred ceremonies in the magical valley and never had anyone seen any trace of this fearsome creature. The pool was also said to be magical, to hold powers that could turn a human into something else or draw a person into its depths, never to be seen again. Brenn had no idea how the stories and legends had started. The people of his village laughed at them, though not one member of his pride had ever dared to enter the bottomless basin, as they called it, and test its waters.

He kneeled on the bank and gazed at his reflection on the smooth, glass-like surface. His face looked tired, shadows tainting the delicate skin beneath his green eyes. His long black hair was stringy, caked with blood from his battle and dusty from days of traveling. Blood from his battle wounds

1

was also clinging to his chest, shoulders, arms, and legs. For a moment, his features changed. His lion fought to surface. It was tempting, oh so tempting. His lion was stronger, and could easily complete the journey. His fatigue would fade, his battle wounds heal. Shaking his head wildly, he forced the urge to shift from his mind, his features returning to human. The curse placed upon him and all the members of his pride forbade them to shift. He would lose all semblance of humanity and be nothing but a fierce beast incapable of ever shifting back into his human.

Several generations after the sorcerer had initiated the curse, one of the members of the pride, not believing that it was real, had shifted. The young man had become a raging lion that tried to attack even his own people. His parents and siblings were devastated, afraid Sandio would be slain and gone forever. Though Sandio had lost his humanity, they hoped that one day the curse would be lifted and he could return to them. Brenn and several other warriors on leave from the king's legion had driven the lion out of the village and into the mountains. The lion had not returned to the village, but several members of the pride had spotted him while hunting. Sandio's parents were always relieved when someone reported having seen their son.

Thinking about Sandio brought Brenn's last battle to mind. Not long before he had reached the base of the mountain hiding the enchanted valley, two dryons had attacked him. Dryons were carnivorous creatures. They were large, feared by all, and easily towered over humans. The drool from their maws touching a human's skin would cause a slow, agonizing death as the poison was absorbed through their skin into their bloodstream. Their long tail was their weapon. Thick and very strong, it was spiked. Their body shape was similar to that of a lion, but their legs much bigger, their feet huge. They were difficult to kill, their scaly skin so hard, it was as if it were made of metal. They could also hide easily, as their skin would take on the same color of the foliage behind which they were hiding, enabling them to ultimately surprise their prey.

It had been no easy feat to battle two of the beasts, to avoid their poisonous drool and damaging tails. The only way to kill them was to thrust a sword between their eyes, a hard task because it meant getting close to their drooling maws. He had not killed either one, but he had managed to escape when the dryons were distracted by a korobeast. With their attention diverted to one of their natural food sources, Brenn was left with an open path up the ridge, then down to the magical valley below.

Normally he would have avoided that route, as the valley was sacred to his people, but the magic of the valley kept predators out, and he had no other option but to cross the ridge and ride down into the valley. He carefully mounted his horse and spurred him on, finally making it to the valley as the moons rose fully in the sky.

Brenn approached the pool in the center of the valley. The waterfall feeding it looked like a wall of blue satin threaded with silver. It gushed over rocks up above and surged and plunged into the bottomless pool. Frogs croaking nearby added to the magical sounds. Fronds of forest-green plants swayed gently at its sides. The night air was rife with the nectar-sweet smell of flowers.

He gazed into the water. It was as clear as the tears of a goddess. Not that he had ever seen those tears, but he presumed they were crystal clear. An unusual humming sound reached his ears. He looked up and saw dozens of tiny purple birds descend to suck nectar from the flowers. He knelt and cupped his hands, only hesitating a moment before bringing a taste of the sweet water to his mouth. A heady calm settled over his weary body as if he had spent the evening in

Tarn's tavern drinking his great mead. He splashed some of the icy water on his face and neck to dispel the intoxicating effect.

Then he saw her... Grabbing the base of his cloak, Brenn quickly wiped the water from his eyes. He shook his head in disbelief. This woman, this dainty, naked nymph rising from the water, was not what the legends spoke of. Her body glowed in the moonlight, a halo of unruly raven hair framing an exquisite face and cascading down to her trim waist. Her full, luscious lips parted in song, hypnotizing him, beckoning him to come to her...begging him to take her. The gods were smiling upon him again with the gift of this ravishing creature.

The gaze of her luminous eyes caught his, entrancing him. He wasted no time approaching the nymph. Unclasping his cloak and dropping it to the grass, he kicked off his boots and removed his armor, and only wearing his codpiece and belt, he waded into the water. Any willpower he might have had was now lost to the pure lust reflected in the cool violet depths of her eyes. His body was on fire with a need that only this temptress could satisfy.

She took him by the hand. Her touch was like lightning, sending shockwaves of lust and anticipation through his fevered body. Her small hands reached up and rested on his shoulders, then lightly pushed him down into the cleansing water. Her velvety fingers feathered through his hair, washing out the grime. Her hands gently moved to his arms and chest, setting fire to his skin. Between the stimulating effect of the water and the trail of fire her hands blazed across his skin, he, a mighty warrior, was now her willing captive.

She led him out of the water to the bank of the enchanted pool and lay down upon the soft grass. Her raven hair splayed out around her, the ambient light of the full moons reflecting upon her, giving her skin a shimmering silvery sheen. The small scales dotting her forehead and temples fascinated him. They ran down the side of her face, to her neck and shoulders, causing her skin to glow like fire opals in the soft light of the moons. The aureoles surrounding her nipples had darker shiny scales. His gaze traveled from her scale-covered cleavage to where it tapered to her abdomen. He had never seen a woman like her. Not even the women from the Nikalia tribe could match her beauty. The Nikalia tribe's women were fair, their hair like moonlight, their eyes the deep blue color of the zanakel flower, their skin the palest blue, and were considered the most beautiful women on Ierilia. No, his nymph was magical, as if from another world.

Brenn needed no words of encouragement. Swiftly, he lay beside her and cupped her face in his hands. He tilted her chin and sampled her inviting lips. She tasted of the sweet nectar of the tea flowers that covered the valley. She devoured him, taking control like a lioness, teasing and nipping at his lips, deepening the kiss until his very soul quaked with the need to make her his.

Brenn broke the kiss. He needed to touch her…to taste his wanton little water sprite. He fought to regain control and give her the pleasure she so desired. Pushing her tenderly back down upon the grass, he traced the outline of her lips with his finger, then down to the rosy peaks of her voluptuous breasts. He was surprised at the silky softness of her scales. Lowering his head, he first took one dusky tip in his mouth, then the other, nipping and sucking until she writhed with pleasure. Her soft moans encouraged him as he trailed kisses down her taut stomach and shapely hips, tantalizing her with his lips as he made his way to the treasure he sought. Carefully he parted her legs, bringing his lips to her soft mound to taste the sweet ambrosia of her arousal. His mouth locked on the swollen bud of her clit, sucking hard as he slipped his finger into the depths of her pussy.

He heard her gasp with the pleasure of it, her body arching like a strung bow to meet his exquisite torture. Her opening was tight, so tight that two fingers barely fit. He moved his fingers back and forth until he felt the warmth of her juices begin to flow. He had her spiraling into the unknown, yearning and aching for the release only he, her captive warrior, could give. Her hips bucked in unison to the melody his tongue played across her clit and the onslaught of his fingers.

The raging storm he had created within her continued to build until it erupted into a tempest. She screamed her release as wave after wave of pleasure pummeled her body. Brenn continued his torture, lapping hungrily at her sweet cream while the spasms lashed his fingers. Her nimble fingers unclasped his belt and drew off his codpiece, releasing his cock. He gasped as her warm hand encased his erection, as she began to move the skin back and forth. Jolts shot through his cock to his pulsing veins, like lightning in a storm. Brenn was certainly not a virgin, but never in his life had he felt such lust.

He could handle no more. His desire built up to the boiling point. Against her protest, he removed her hand from the aching hardness of his cock and captured her mouth in a kiss. He raised his head for a moment, gazing upon her indescribable beauty, a loveliness that only mythical tales spoke of. He dropped down beside her, capturing her mouth again. The taste of his sweet siren's lips was more intoxicating than the water he had sampled. His mind spun. His heart pounded in his chest.

She pushed him backward and sideways to the grass and slid her body on top of his, straddling him across his abdomen, her aggressiveness an aphrodisiac that kept him securely under her spell. His cock jumped and pulsed against the soft touch of her wet pussy. She was clearly in control of him now—determined to pleasure herself and her warrior as she saw fit. She ran her fingers across his muscular chest. Slowly she explored the strong muscles of his chest, kissing and caressing his heated skin. The feather-light touch of her fingertips across his chest sent tingling ripples all the way to his core. Shockwaves of pleasure shook him with each touch of her hand and each kiss from her lips.

The feel of her wet slit grinding against his cock was too much. She was driving him to the point of insanity. He needed to feel her velvety folds squeezing tight around him. He grabbed her shapely hips, raising her slightly. Her hands encircled his cock, guiding the throbbing heat to her slick entrance. With one thrust he buried himself in her. She gasped as his engorged cock broke through the barrier and filled her.

Too late, he realized his mistake. His temptress was a virgin. Brenn stilled his movement and pulled her down to kiss her deeply. He slipped his hand between them and teased her clit until she relaxed against him, her skin now as hot as molten lava, matching the heat of his own. Their bodies moved in unison, slowly at first as he let her become accustomed to the invasion of never-before claimed territory.

He felt the heat of passion build as she impaled herself upon him, riding him, harder and deeper, each thrust of her hips bringing him closer to release. Brenn squeezed her hips, meeting her with the same reckless abandon. He watched her throw her head back, her eyes suddenly glowing a vivid purple, and he thought he saw flashes of amber as if the heat of a volcano had erupted within her body.

Her pussy spasmed and squeezed his cock. Brenn groaned, thrusting deeper and deeper into her as he exploded.

Sated and panting from the pleasure he had given her, she collapsed against him.

After catching his breath from their passionate exertion, Brenn stood with his nymph nestled in his arms. He carried her to the enchanted pool and waded into the cool water to help her soothe the ache of their joining. Gradually she slid down his body, the touch of her skin igniting a slow burn again.

Kissing her lips, he ran his hands down to her parted thighs and carefully delved his fingers into her cleft. She moaned and tilted her hips, allowing him easier access to her folds. He massaged her until she gasped and her body shuddered in release. She wrapped her arms around his neck and anchored her legs around his hips, impaling herself on his cock once more.

Brenn took her gently this time, allowing their passion to engulf them. When her muscles tightened and spasmed around him, he groaned at the exquisite feel of it. He quickened his pace as he kissed her alluring lips. She released his lips, trailing kisses along his jaw, then down to his neck and shoulder. Her teeth closed around the sensitive area at the base of his neck and shoulder, sending sparks of heat all the way to his cock. His body on fire, he pumped harder into her tight folds as his cock spasmed and released inside her.

Kissing her one more time, he lifted her in his arms and to the bank of the pool where they had made love the first time. Lying down with her still in his arms, he looked up at the moons and stars in the night sky, silently thanking the gods for the precious gift they had given him.

Brenn shifted to his side, bringing her with him to lay her completely in their grassy nest. He propped himself up on one elbow to drink in the beauty of this bewitching woman. Her eyes, again a cool violet, held a sadness and longing that pierced his soul. She tried to speak, but only the enchanting song she sang earlier came from her sweet lips. Brenn silenced her parted lips with a kiss and pulled her close. He did not care what sort of magick had brought her to him, but he knew he would never let her go.

Ciara's heart filled with love for her willing warrior, but she knew she would have to leave him. Emptiness gripped her soul with the realization that what she wanted could only be a dream. A sigh escaped her lips. At least she had this night to spend with her handsome lover.

She rose from the velvety bed of grass, gazing down at the handsome man still sleeping soundly. He had captured her heart as no other man could. She memorized each feature— his long black hair, the chiseled nose, the full lips that had pleasured her so thoroughly throughout the night. She must have one last kiss before the suns rose. Kneeling beside him, she lightly brushed her lips against his.

The delicate touch of her lips stirred him. His arms snaked around her, pulling her closer as he deepened their kiss and reignited their passion.

Ciara pushed against him, pulling her lips away from his. The suns were peeking over the horizon, telling her that her time was up. Tears streamed down her face as the transformation began. She knew her eyes mirrored the pain in her soul and she hoped her warrior would understand what was happening.

The change began. A large violet tear dropped from her dragon's eye. She caught it in her hand and felt a shard of her soul melding into the tear, turning it into hard crystal. The gem dropped to the grass as her dragon took over her body. She had found her lifemate, but they could never be completely together. Cewrick, the sorcerer, had made that impossible.

Her lips formed into a small, sad smile. Though Cewrick had cursed her to live her life as a dragon, bound her to the bottomless basin, he had no knowledge that if she ever laid eyes upon her lifemate, she could briefly shed her dragon and spend a short period as her human.

Sadness overwhelmed her as she thought about her clan, forever cursed to serve Cewrick, their humanity ultimately removed, forced to fly the skies as black, much-feared dragons to do his bidding. She had escaped before Cewrick's magick could touch her soul, but not fast enough, so he had still placed a curse on her as she crossed the summit to descend into the magical realm below.

For so many years she had prayed for the prophecy of the goddess to come true. Not long after she had made the pool her home, she was in deep despair. The anguish of living in the pool for all eternity had torn at her heart and soul. She had felt so helpless, incapable of even ending her life. Then, one day when she had ventured briefly out of the pool, she had rested below a tree, and the goddess had spoken to her.

Do not despair, child. A warrior will come, one that will help you. We will guide your lifemate to you.

But so much time had passed, days and nights blending, that she had thought the voice a dream.

As she had rested in the depths of the pool, she had hardly believed it when she saw his face through the water. Her heart had sped up in the hope that this man could release her from spending her life in this valley and the pool. He was the first to ever dare drink from the water. As she had surfaced, gazed upon his handsome face, she had begun to shift to her human form and had known immediately that the gods had sent this man to rescue her from bondage.

Now she was free to at least guard her lifemate. The curse could never be entirely removed until Cewrick was stripped of his magick. All Brenn had to do was whisper her name, and she would be able to spread her wings and escape from the pool and this valley to find him.

Brenn's eyes widened as his siren's body began to take on a different shape. He reached for her hand, not wanting to let her go, but it was too late. The dragon turned from him and slithered into the cool water of the basin. *No... This cannot be.* His heart was ripped from him as the dragon disappeared into the water.

His gaze rested one last time upon the grass where his temptress had once stood. A glint in the sunlight caught his eye. Brenn knelt and picked up one lone gem in the shape of a tear. Within the sparkling crystal was a reflection of his seductive sprite. His beautiful nymph had left him a sliver of her soul.

Reaching into his saddlebag, he took out a small leather pouch that held a few coins. He undid the string, shook the coins out of it, and threw them into the saddlebag. Then he placed the crystal tear inside it and tied the string around his neck.

All tiredness had left his body, and his wounds from the battle with the dryons were healed. He felt refreshed and full of vigor, ready to resume his journey home to his village.

After he had dressed, he mounted his horse. Suddenly he felt a heated tingle warming his skin beneath the pouch. Instinctively, he reached up to grasp it, wondering what it was. Then he thought he heard a whisper, or was it the wind? Did he imagine it?

I will always be there for you when you need me, my love. All you need to do to summon me is to hold the crystal in your hand and say my name. I am Ciara, your guardian. We have bonded. I am forever yours.

CHAPTER ONE

T/The black stallion snorted impatiently, startling Brenn out of his thoughts. The horse, like himself, was invigorated by drinking from the magical pool. Like his master, the stallion was eager to head for home. Brenn had owned him since boyhood and had named him Atom for his speed. He flicked the reins and Atom took off.

As they slowly ascended the steep path to the top of the mountain, Brenn's mind again wandered to his experience in the pool. Had it been a dream? His feverish imagination? The crystal within the pouch belied that thought. He wanted to take it out and look at it again, but he withstood the temptation. He needed to concentrate on the road home, on returning to his family. His dreams and fantasies could wait until later.

The trek up to the crest of the mountain was slow but easy. The mountainside was just as enchanted as the pool where he had rested. The crimson leaves of the woodbine trees rustled in the cool breeze as they passed through them. Beneath them, gloweed covered the ground. Deep red phrage bushes in full bloom were abundant, as were the tiny blue imperial tea flowers. Occasionally he heard the sweet sound of the nyctea birds singing as they flew through the sky, and the scuttle of antuars, tiny six-legged furry animals. They were cute and, if people could catch one, were kept as pets. At times, one or two sat on a branch to look at the human and horse invading their territory. It was tempting to take one home, but it was forbidden to take anything from the enchanted valley and surrounding mountains. Sometimes an antuar would venture to the other side of the mountain and the valley below. Brenn's sister had one for a pet. Shanina had tamed it and called it Twinkle because its downy green fur seemed to shimmer. Brenn had often wondered if Twinkle had magical abilities.

He almost hated leaving this beautiful paradise. It was not foreign to him. It was sacred to their pride. It was where the gods and goddesses resided. Many ceremonies had been performed in the enchanted valley. Joining ceremonies, where the couple's bodies were painted with beautiful designs of birds, flowers, and foliage. The passing into the realm of dreams of one of their elders — the ashes were spread around the pool, and they would chant and sing ceremonial songs for three nights and days, feast and dance. The birth of a baby, the infant taken to the enchanted valley by the parents and grandparents to be introduced to the gods, and other traditional ceremonies.

By late evening, he had almost reached the mountain's crest. On the other side, down in the valley, was his village. The trek to it was difficult, fraught with danger from cave dwellers, black dragons, and other predators.

Though he was anxious to return home swiftly, he urged Atom farther up the path to a small clearing along the banks of a stream, perfect for setting up a camp for the night. He dismounted and rubbed Atom's head from his ears to his snout, speaking softly to his loyal mount. After one last pat to Atom's flank, he let him graze along the edge of the water.

Kneeling by the stream, Brenn cupped his hands in the cool

water and brought it to his mouth for a drink. For a moment, he allowed the memory of Ciara, her beautiful face, mesmerizing violet eyes, her perfect alabaster body, their union, if it had even been real. Then the words he had heard in his mind, *I will always be there if you need me.* Had she really shifted into a dragon? He felt so confused. She had stolen a part of his soul, his heart—but had he conjured up an image of his deepest wishes, the dream woman and lifemate for whom he longed?

Unconsciously, he reached for the pouch and held it for a moment. An intense tingling ran from his fingertips and up his arm. Yanking his hand away, he stood briskly and proceeded to set up camp for the night. The journey the next day would not be so pleasant, as the path bordered near caves inhabited by the Laeturians, a mountain tribe that hunted quartz lions and other creatures for sport and as a rite of passage to adulthood.

He gathered some wood and started a campfire, then laid out his bedroll. It would be a cool, clear night, and the fire would help dispel some of the chill. He checked Atom one more time and tied his tether to a tree close by, giving his horse plenty of room to graze on the sweet grass by the water's edge. Sitting by the campfire, he nibbled on some dried meat and berries, took a swig of water from his waterskin, then lay down on his bedroll to sleep under the crimson canopy of the trees.

A flash of silvery skin. A soft sigh of pleasure. A hand trailing through his hair, along the ridge of his jaw, down to his chest where the pouch lay. "I will always be there if you need me." Her soft voice whispered to him. Her hand toyed with the leather pouch. A feather-light string of kisses seared his skin as her lips followed the path her fingers had taken. Her silken hair brushed his chest as she turned her head to rest there. Brenn moaned and shifted to place his arms around his temptress, but all his arms met was a hollow space where she should be.

Brenn woke with a start to the intense tingling he was beginning to associate with the crystal in the pouch resting on his chest. His hand clasped the pouch. Even at rest, he was haunted by her; his soul ripped in half by a specter. He dropped the pouch to his chest, left his bedroll, and waded into the stream to cool his skin and wake himself up for the rest of his journey home.

He finished washing, then left the stream to dress and break up camp. After stowing his gear in his saddlebags, he untied Atom's tether and mounted his stallion. He spurred Atom back to the path home.

It would be a short, uneventful ride to the summit. The legends of the enchanted pool kept predators and creatures at bay on that side of the mountain. There were many that were not brave enough to rile the creature rumored to make the pool its home.

Winding through the trees along the path, Brenn felt the change in his stallion's steps as the road started taking a sharper incline. He urged Atom onward as they broke through the trees and reached the summit.

He halted Atom, and they stood there for a minute, gazing down at the valley. His village would be barely visible from that far up, but he should be able to see smoke spiraling up from chimneys and cooking fires, and some activity.

There was nothing. No smoke, no movement. The area where his village once stood was blackened, like the charred crystals mined from the earth and rocks along the foothills of the mountain. The valley below was utterly silent. Sounds should have drifted to his ears, the laughter of children, women singing, men at work, echoing throughout the valley.

The intense silence sent a terrifying message to his heart.

Burned. Gone. His stomach somersaulted, tied itself into knots, and his heart beat a staccato rhythm that echoed in his ears. His throat contracted at the thought that everyone had perished.

Praying to the gods for an uneventful trip down the treacherous path, he kicked his heels into Atom's sides to spark him into action. They crossed the summit and pushed through the trees to the path on the other side.

The trees were not quite as abundant, the crimson of the leaves darker, almost blood red. The bark and limbs were gnarled and so dark they were almost obsidian in color. The landscape gave off an air of foreboding that matched the creatures that hid within it.

Frustrated at the difficulty of navigating the downward path, he nudged Atom, and they began their descent. Not fast enough for Brenn, but he could not endanger his horse or himself.

It seemed to take forever to get to the base of the mountain. It was near noon when he could finally spur Atom into a gallop and head toward his village.

Close to sunset, they arrived at Xynnar. Atom reared, whinnying. Brenn leaned forward to soothe the horse, patting him on the head and whispering calming words. Atom settled and stood, though still snorting.

Pushing onward, he broke through the copse of trees surrounding his village, but there was nothing. No smoke spiraling up from chimneys on the houses fashioned from mud bricks. No children playing or women going about their daily activities. No warriors practicing in the field. All Brenn saw was a blackened expanse. What had once been his village was gone, burned to the ground. Anger and fear consumed him. Fear of what had happened to his family, his father and mother, his sister, to the other people of his pride. Anger at who or what had done this burst through him. For the first time in his life, both man and beast became one with a roar of agony so intense it echoed throughout the valley.

Brenn gazed at the destruction. From the top of the mountain, it had not been that visible, but now he could see the damage clearly. There was not a dwelling left standing. Piles of black debris lay scattered on the ashes. He spurred Atom on. They slowly walked through the village, but he saw no charred bodies. No remains. Where was his family? Where were all the other occupants? There was no sign of blood. What had happened there? His heart shredded with fear for his family and the members of his pride. They had lived in peace in their valley for so many years. What or who had invaded their territory?

The war he had just returned from had been resolved and ended. It was a war far away, not involving his pride, a battle between two regents, Lord Quadra, ruler of Nasteria, and Lord Klubotah, ruler of Drapingo. Lord Quadra, jealous of the neighboring county's fertile valley that was rich in orchards and mining, coveted his neighbor's wealth. He had invaded, and a reign of terror had ensued, causing much bloodshed. King Biryn was a fair ruler but tolerated no war between clans, so he had dispatched his army, led by his general, Brenn. The fighting had lasted several months, finally ending with the capture of Lord Quadra, now in custody and confined to the dungeons beneath the royal palace and awaiting trial by fire.

When Brenn was young, he had no wish to become a miner like his father. He had always dreamed of becoming a warrior and had enlisted in the army of King Biryn, ruler of their planet. He and Biryn had met as boys, the king more a brother than a friend or ruler. Biryn did not have to do much prodding to talk him into joining. The adventure and glory wooed him long before they had met. He had learned fast and swiftly advanced up the ranks to general. Now that the war was over, he was on leave, allowed a reprieve of several moons to rest from the fighting.

The planet was once again at peace. He had not heard of more discord. If there were, the king's messenger birds would have sought him out and delivered the order for him to return to the palace with full speed. And if it were urgent, the king would have sent a hovercraft for him.

So what had happened to his home? His pride had never been involved in any conflict. His magical encounter — or dream — receded into the furthest recesses of his mind, completely displaced by his anger and worry. He continued on through the village but found no evidence of the cause of the destruction.

Dismounting, still holding tight onto the reins because Atom was restless, he walked to the pile of charred remains that used to be his childhood home and felt it. Cold. *How long ago did this happen?* There was no evidence of any fighting, no corpses. Had everyone been captured? Most of the older members of his pride were not skilled fighters unless they called out their lion, and that was forbidden. All the younger men of his pride were trained as ground and space warriors, but they were not experienced. The young men on Ierilia were called to training camp when they reached the age of eighteen. They would train for six moons, and some that excelled would be asked if they wanted to enlist. If there were ever a massive invasion, the others would be called to serve their king.

Ripping his gaze away from the ashes, he mounted his horse, deciding to scout the surrounding forest to look for survivors, some kind of evidence, for bodies, though his stomach knotted even tighter at the thought of finding his parents and sister dead and mutilated.

Grinding his teeth together, his mouth a tight line, he began his search. He was tempted to get off his horse, but that could be dangerous. He was safer on Atom, though predators could also be lurking in the trees up above, he suddenly realized. He scanned the dense foliage. It was difficult to spot anything among the thick, hairy leaves. The shrubbery on the ground, too, could hide anything or anyone.

He saw nothing. There were no tracks on the ground. Not a sign of anything. After he had scouted for a few hours and circled several times, he was about to give up when Atom reared and a figure emerged from a hollow tree. Instantly drawing his sword, Brenn was ready, not to kill, but to capture whoever or whatever it was.

"Brenn, no, it is me," a man shouted.

CHAPTER TWO

Brenn calmed Atom and sheathed his sword. He had recognized that voice—it belonged to Ivran, his best friend. He dismounted and ran to embrace Ivran. Swallowing hard to get rid of the lump in his throat, he stepped back, still holding Ivran by the shoulders. "Ivran, my friend, what has happened here?"

Tears ran unashamedly down Ivran's sooty face. His normally tidy, long blond hair was dirty and unkempt, his tunic torn. "They came and took them." He stopped as sobs shook his muscular frame. "Abducted them all—my mate, my baby, everyone. We fought, but it was futile. I am the only one that managed to escape because I had just returned from a fishing expedition. Their weapons are so much more advanced from ours. They did not kill any of our men, women, or children. The weapons they fired caused unconsciousness. I hid among the shrubbery, then tried to get to my house, but it was of no use."

"Calm down, Ivran. You are not making any sense. Sit down. Let me get you some eldalas spirit." He ran to Atom and took a flask from his saddlebag, then quickly returned to Ivran and held it to his lips. The fiery liquid calmed him. "Now tell me. Who or what did this?"

"Spaceships, from Toubos. By the gods, I have never seen such ugly people, Brenn, if you can even call them people. They are inhuman. They are hideous. They took everyone away in their ships," Ivran said, his voice still shaky.

"Toubos? I thought our king had friendly relations with the rulers of that planet."

"That is all I can tell you."

"So they took them away. Where to? To their planet? But why?" Brenn asked, though he knew Ivran would not have the answer. "How many ships?"

Ivran shook his head. "I'm not sure. One hovered over our village, but I saw a couple more, high up above. After the ship had ascended, they fired their weapons and set the village ablaze."

Brenn swore under his breath. Everything had been as it should on his travels home after he had left the Clyss. No attacks, everything normal. Why the sudden interest in their realm? The Toubosians had sent several ships, but only one craft had attacked the village and abducted all the occupants? During his travels, he had heard nothing, no rumors of alien attacks, of spaceship sightings. Would they really send several ships to capture the people from one village? Had the ships returned to Toubos? He doubted it. He had a feeling the ships were hiding somewhere within the Sucronian Mountains near Cewrick's castle — planning another attack?

Were the Toubosians in league with Cewrick, the evil sorcerer who had placed the curse on all shifters? The sorcerer's castle stood on the highest peak in the center of the Sucronian Mountains, a forbidden mountain range. No one dared to approach it. At the base of the mountains was the Forbidden Forest. Its trees were said to have been bespelled by Cewrick and would kill anything or anyone treading the ground below. Large black dragons guarded the castle, along with urcals, giant birds with wingspans as wide as the road in his village. They, too, were black. They had bright orange beaks that were curved and very sharp. Their claws were so big; they could easily swoop up several horses at once. Their talons were the length of a man's arm, their eyes glowing like embers.

They had all seen the dragons and the birds as they circled above the Forbidden Forest. Brenn's father, Yartah, the alpha of their pride, and some of the warriors, including Brenn, had ventured to the edge of the forest when one of their young women had suddenly gone missing. When Huf, a young warrior, rode ahead into the forest, one of the monstrous birds had plucked him and the horse from between the trees and disappeared with them.

After that tragic event, Yartah had doubly enforced the rules. No one was allowed to venture near the forest. Brenn did not think after what had happened that anyone would even dare, but one never knew what young people would do. The youngsters thought themselves invincible. The only thing that seemed to scare them was the curse — if they shifted, which usually surfaced during puberty, they would remain a lion forever and lose all humanity.

He turned his attention back to Ivran. His friend was distraught, barely holding onto his human form, his lion fighting to burst free.

"Ivran, do not shift! Remember the curse. Calm yourself. You cannot do any good if you lose your humanity. You will even forget you have a mate and child. Let us find shelter for the night. We will continue our search after we're both rested."

Brenn helped Ivran mount Atom, then took the reins and led them to an outcrop of rocks along the banks of the river. There they would have shelter from the elements, fresh fish to eat, and water to refill his waterskin.

He tethered Atom to a tree, then helped Ivran dismount

and handed him a knife. "You catch some fish, and I will set up camp and gather some firewood."

He watched Ivran carve a spear from a tree branch, then wade into the water to spear the fish. Fishing would help Ivran keep himself under control and, Brenn hoped, take his mind off his missing mate and new baby.

Turning away from Ivran, Brenn grabbed his gear from the saddlebags and began to set up camp under the outcrop. He walked to the edge of the forest to gather firewood, then returned, and after building a tinder nest, he rubbed two sticks together to ignite it. As soon as he had a flame, he began adding wood. Within a few minutes, the smoldering kindling set the wood ablaze.

Ivran returned holding up several large makulel, a fish they often caught and cooked for their evening meals. "Good job, Ivran," Brenn complimented him as he took the fish, wrapped them in broad leaves, then placed them on a log to roast. Soon the smell of the roasting fish wafted through the air, making their stomachs rumble.

"At least we'll have food for tonight and maybe the morning. It is a shame that even our vineyards and orchards were destroyed. We'll have to find fruit during our travels."

"Travels?" Ivran asked.

"Yes. We need to travel to the capital and speak to King Biryn. Our ruler needs to be informed about this. Who knows what the Toubosians are planning."

"I need to search for my mate and child," Ivran said.

"Friend, what can you and I do against the Toubosians and their ships? The king has his own fleet of spaceships and space warriors. We are useless with just a sword to wield. There's something more behind this. I have thought about it, and I have a feeling they are hiding within the Sucronian Mountains, and that they are in league with Cewrick. This is a battle that needs more than just us two. I understand your fear for your loved ones. I fear for my family, too, and the rest of our people. But we have to be sensible. I love you, Ivran. You are more than a friend. We grew up together, and we are more like brothers, the brother I never had, and my heart bleeds for you as it bleeds for my family. Please, listen to a warrior's council."

Ivran nodded. "I hear you. We are like brothers, now and forever. I will listen to you."

"Good. We fear the worst, but if the Toubosians were going to kill our people, they would have annihilated them when they destroyed our village and our crops. I believe our loved ones and the other members of our pride are very much alive and being kept so for a reason. What that reason is, only the gods and goddesses know." Brenn sighed and handed Ivran his flask. "We will leave at first light after we eat. The first village is a three-hour ride to the east, and Atom will have to slow down while carrying both of us. We need to get you a horse, too. I did not see any of our cattle or horses. Did they take our livestock, too?"

"Our livestock scattered, too. As they fled, they broke the fences. As for buying a horse, I have no coins, nothing to trade. We could try and find our horses tomorrow morning."

"That will take too much time. I will buy you a horse. Not to worry," Brenn reassured him. Brenn slid his knife under two of the roasting fish and held them out to his friend. Ivran carefully took one and unwrapped it. The scent of the cooked fish made Brenn's mouth water. He had not eaten anything since the dried meat and berries from the night before. He managed a grin. "I'm carrying enough reward from the last victory to buy us a herd of horses. Now let us eat and then get some rest. The fire should burn until daylight." Unwrapping his own fish, he took a succulent piece of the flesh and popped it into his mouth.

Brenn stopped eating as he heard a rustling noise coming

from a bush near their camp. "Hear that?"

Ivran gazed at the nearby brush and trees.

A louder noise close by grabbed their attention. Setting their fish aside, they stood, ready to do battle. It could be a small animal, but with recent events, both men were not taking any chances.

"Here take this," Brenn said as he handed Ivran his knife. He turned to unsheathe his sword when he felt something grab his leg and run up the length of his body to settle in the crook of his shoulder. Its furry body trembled as it made *brtttt* noises while nuzzling the side of his face.

"Twink!" he said as he grabbed his sister's beloved pet and cuddled him close to his chest. "It is okay, Twink, I've got you. Shanina will be so glad you are safe." He rubbed Twinkle's ears and neck while soothing the creature as he thought of his beautiful sister, his heart heavy with sadness.

Ivran sat back down to finish his dinner. "Fierce little beast."

Brenn chuckled and offered a bite of fish to Twink. "Better finish our supper and rest up for tomorrow."

Brenn waited until Ivran slept before he relaxed near the fire, the hilt of his sword in his hand. Twinkle had finally settled in to sleep, curled up in a ball on his cloak, but rest did not come easy for Brenn. Once Ivran had settled down, he could think more clearly, and he mapped out their route in his mind.

Through all the turmoil of that day, he had almost forgotten about the pouch that hung from his neck. His free hand reached to hold it. The familiar tingling set his hand on fire and ran up his arm. He was tempted to take out the crystal and say her name, as she had told him. But what could she do to help? That was if she were even real and if it had truly happened, which he still questioned. But the crystal teardrop was real, and it was magical — of that he had no doubt.

His thoughts became jumbled, the plan for their travels

mixing with the memories of his fantasy. The heat of the fire made him drowsy, and he began to drift off into a restless slumber, sleep filled with dreams about aliens, spacecraft, his family, and his nymph beckoning him.

Ciara lay beside the pool, her thoughts drifting back to so long ago. How many moons had it been? How many centuries? She had lost count. Too many.

Cewrick had forced the change upon her, as well as the other dragons of her clan, taking all of them prisoner, but her mind and that of her cousin Taylith were not completely erased. Somehow, a semblance of their humanity had remained. They had managed to elude their captors. With their village destroyed and their clan under Cewrick's spell, they had no choice but to make their escape to the Clyss Valley in the Crimson Realm.

Taylith had been wounded so badly he could not take flight, so they had to make their way on foot through the thick forest and up the treacherous, steep mountain path.

When Cewrick's minions finally overtook them just before they reached the summit of the mountain, Taylith had sacrificed himself to ensure her escape. Her cousin had urged her on and told her only she could save them all now. With a heavy heart, she had left him knowing he would be captured by the black dragons. She had prayed to the gods and goddesses to save him from harm, to at least allow him to live, even if he were to become one of the sorcerer's black dragon slaves.

Once she had reached the summit and stepped over the sacred threshold, where she knew she would be safe, she had turned to see Taylith, held by a black dragon, high up in the sky. Violet dragon tears dripped to the ground as she made her way down the mountain to the valley to the pool. She did not notice that as each tear soaked the soil, a beautiful purple flower instantly sprouted and was in full bloom in seconds. She had arrived at the pool and entered it, her heart heavy with sorrow for her cousin, her family, and her friends, not realizing that the pool would trap her. The magic of the water had bound her dragon to the valley.

Cewrick's army was made up of mindless creatures to do his bidding. His discovery of the soul shards had set him on a path of destruction that had ripped her world apart. He had gained control of her clan by capturing the younglings. The adults were willing to sacrifice their lives by giving up their soul shards for the freedom of their young. It had been a futile sacrifice. Not only did Cewrick take their soul shards, but he also captured the adults.

After claiming the soul shards from the adults, the sorcerer weaved a spell that tore through infants and adults alike, forcing a change so painful it killed many of them. For those from whom Cewrick had claimed their souls, their beautiful jewel tones had turned as black as pitch. Their scales changed shape into pointed quills, and their teeth elongated to protrude from their maws, dripping an acid so harsh it could eat through armor. They had lost all humanity.

Cewrick had added to his army, but he was not satisfied. He needed Ciara, a sorceress in her own right, and she knew he would not cease to hunt her. Without her soul shard, his magical powers were not complete. But her soul shard was finally lost to him forever. The gods had sent her a lifemate, the one only meant for her. Only he could help free her now.

The key to releasing her from Cewrick's spell was her soul shard. She knew it to the depth of her being. When Brenn had touched the waters of the Clyss, his soul had reached out to hers. Their connection was so intense that it had forced her body to shift into human form with a lust so profound she had to take the human that sparked it. Her instincts had taken over as she captured the man under her siren's spell.

He had scorched her soul into awakening, and for the first time in centuries, she could shift into her human. Even though she could not hold the form for a long period, it had allowed her time enough to transfer a sliver of her soul to the shard.

The dragon rested her head on her forelegs, watching the water from the falls spill into the pool below. She gazed at her reflection on the surface of the smooth waters of the pool. Her violet scales glowed with a silvery sheen under the light of Ierilia's four moons, her eyes a deep shade of purple sadness, moist with unshed tears.

Ciara ached to touch her warrior again. She could feel Brenn's fingers close around her soul shard, her reptilian body tingling with fire to change. If he would just say her name, she could be freed from Clyss Valley to comfort him as her human, even if only for a few hours while the moons hung heavy in the sky, and during daylight, her dragon could guard him. Each time he touched or clasped the pouch around his neck, their connection grew stronger.

She felt everything that tore him asunder — his horrific pain and loss when he came upon his demolished village ripped through her. She shared his despair, her inability to help him gnawing at her heart.

Brenn was her lifemate. Her soul shard was in his keeping as it should be, but how could that be? He was a lion with a soul as fierce as the animal inside him. A mating as profound as theirs had never happened in her lifetime, nor had one ever been written about. Lions and dragons did not mate, much less become lifemates. Deep inside she knew the truth — their souls were bound, and she accepted it. If Brenn did not accept the deep meaning of their mating and what her soul shard truly was, she would be trapped in her dragon form for eternity.

CHAPTER THREE

Brenn woke early, well before the twin suns rose in the sky, his body and mind still tired from his travels home. It did not help that his sleep was restless, haunted by dreams of aliens and visions of his hallucination at the magical pool. Yet those visions had been so vivid. He could still picture her in his mind, her beautiful alabaster skin flashing silver in the moonlight, her violet eyes that turned a deep shade of purple with passion as they had made love, her waist-length black hair that had a purple sheen to it.

Gods, she had been so enchanting as she had beckoned him to her. He felt his cock rising, his skin burning with need. He tried to still his lust, but without success.

Glancing at Ivran, who was still fast asleep near the glowing embers of the dying fire, he made his way quickly to the river, hoping the cold water would ease the fire within him. Once there, he took off his garments, waded into the river, and dove into the water. All it did was remind him of their passionate night by the Clyss.

He allowed his imagination to run free as he trod water and clasped his aching erection in his hand, imagining it to be her hand grasping him. He could see her so clearly, her succulent breasts with dark nipples surrounded by a large aureole, erect and taut, beckoning for his lips to taste them. Her slender yet shapely body, wading toward him in the water, enticing him to touch, her hand held out, beckoning him, her long black hair flowing in the soft breeze. His gaze rested on the black triangle beneath her navel, her cleft easily visible as she parted her legs, her clitoris peeking out from between rosy lips. He glanced at her face again, at her tongue moistening her lips, begging for his kiss. He pumped his hand up and down fast and hard, moving the skin of his cock back and forth. His breathing labored, he grasped his cock tighter as his semen burst forth, spilling onto his hand to be rinsed away by the rushing current.

Breathing heavily, he shook his head and dove back into the cold river water. *You are going insane, Brenn. You are lusting after a phantom. Get a grip on yourself.*

He swam for a while, then finally headed back for shore to join Ivran, who had in the meantime woken up and was busy stoking the fire and cooking a coracal he had caught. Twinkle was sitting on a log, feasting on a raw coracal of his own. Really? Had he been in the water that long? Long enough for Ivran to hunt for more fish for breakfast?

After he had dressed, he hurried to the fire and Ivran, his stomach growling. Coracal was a favorite breakfast fish for his family, especially if roasted over an open fire. He noticed the sky clouding over and sighed. The forest was quiet, too still. That meant another storm was brewing. They had been plagued by them recently, the weather much harsher than the regular light rains they usually experienced.

They ate their breakfast in silence, both still coming to terms with the loss of their family and friends.

After eating, they broke camp and loaded what gear they had into Atom's saddlebags.

Brenn carefully placed Twinkle on top of his cloak inside

one of the saddlebags. Twink was used to riding thus with his sister. The little creature chattered at him before curling up into a ball inside the saddlebag.

Brenn turned to Ivran before mounting his horse. "Look at the sky. Cewrick is playing games again. Ierilia has never seen such rain and wind as we have had of late. We will have to travel speedily if we want to beat this storm, but I doubt we will. Arluc is three hours away at least. Atom has a double load to carry, so our journey there will be slower than usual."

"Agreed, I have no wish to be chilled to the bone from a downpour."

Brenn swung himself into the saddle and reached his hand out to help Ivran mount behind him. Turning the reins eastward, he kicked his heels into Atom's side to spur him into a slow and steady trot.

A good hour into their ride, the wind kicked up speed. Churning clouds darkened the suns' rays. There was a sharp flash of light as lightning struck a woodbine, causing its leaves to swirl in the air and the trunk to split in half, and almost instantly following it, slashing torrents of rain poured from the sky, soaking them.

A loud crash of thunder rumbled across the valley, startling Atom into a gallop. Brenn clung to the reins and yelled to Ivran, "Hold on, I will try to restrain him, but we must find shelter while the worst of the storm passes."

Ivran tightened his arms around Brenn's waist, seeming to hold on for dear life to keep himself seated on the horse.

Brenn steered Atom to a hollow yewneedle tree. Their trunks were so big that a tribe of humans on the west end of the valley used them as homes.

Brenn slowed his horse to a stop and waited for Ivran to dismount, then followed quickly behind him. They led Atom into the massive trunk of the tree and settled in to wait out the storm.

Brenn opened his saddlebag, checking on Twinkle—who was still sleeping, curled up in a ball. He pulled his waterskin from the saddlebag, took a long drink, and passed it to Ivran. Both men seated themselves on the ground, facing the opening in the trunk.

Ivran passed the waterskin back to Brenn, wiped the rainwater from his face, then looked at his friend. "This may shelter us from the storm, but I fear we will be trapped and dead if a morcoug decides to shelter here as well."

Morcougs were massive, beastly creatures that lived in caves in the foothills in the valley. They were carnivorous predators, with four rows of razor-sharp teeth. Two spike-shaped teeth jutted far past their bottom jaw. Their hides were so tough that anyone fighting them practically had to hack through it to do any damage, much less kill them. They had small, beady yellow eyes, and their large paws were tipped with claws that could cut through stone. The only way to mortally wound one was to drive a sword through the soft area at the front of the throat and neck, but for a human to reach that area was impossible.

Brenn shivered in revulsion at the thought. "Let us pray to the gods we have an uneventful stay." Morcougs usually stayed away from humans unless they happened upon one unexpectedly, nor would they attack a group of humans unless provoked. The beasts followed herds of korobeast and harteox from the foothills down into the valley to kill for their food. "We saw no sign or tracks of korobeast or harteox, so the morcougs will not be close."

The storm stopped as fast as it had begun. "Let's continue," Brenn said. Taking Atom's reins, he led the horse out into the sunlight, with Ivran following. Brenn inhaled deeply. Though he would welcome a regular light rain, the air was always so fresh after a downpour cleared it of all the dust.

They continued on the path to Arluc. After they had been

riding for a while, Atom suddenly reared and whinnied. "What's wrong, boy?" Brenn said, trying to calm the horse. Ivran hung on to Brenn so tightly to stay seated, he could barely breathe. Atom calmed again, and Brenn slowed him to a walk.

"What spooked him?" Ivran asked.

"No idea. Maybe something in the shrubbery. Perhaps he is tired. I will just let him walk at his own pace for a bit."

"I see korobeast tracks," Ivran pointed out.

"That means there are probably morcougs in the vicinity. Keep your eyes open, friend."

Again, Atom spooked. He reared, and reared again, throwing Ivran to the ground. Brenn tried with all his might to calm the horse.

Suddenly a morcoug jumped onto the track to confront them. Brenn had seen the beasts from a distance while traveling with his legions but never one this close. The monster had probably killed a korobeast and was ready to defend his catch. Brenn shuddered, knowing this would probably be the day he entered his forever dreams. They did not stand a chance of defeating the morcoug with only one sword between them.

Without thinking, Brenn clasped the pouch around his neck, and without even realizing it, he whispered, "Ciara." That familiar tingling heat radiated through his hand, up his arm, and throughout his body. Dropping the pouch, he drew his sword, jumped off Atom, and slapped the horse on his flank so he could find shelter from the beast. "Ivran, hide!" he yelled.

The morcoug towered as high as the trees. Slime drooled from its gaping maw. It was ready to devour him. Brenn did not scare easily, but fear had his heart beating so fast and so hard he felt it almost hitting his ribs.

He was swift and an experienced fighter, but he felt

helpless against the morcoug. Seeing the creature up close, he knew there was no possible way that he, as a human, could reach its neck for the kill. The beast struck out at him. Brenn jumped away from the tremendous claw, avoiding the stream of acidic drool that ran from its mouth. His one advantage was that compared to the monster, he was a speck of dust. The morcoug's size made its movements clumsy.

Brenn stepped backward cautiously, never taking his focus off the animal or its movements. Deep down, he knew he was fighting a losing battle. Even if he took flight, the morcoug would reach out and pluck him up as if he were a berry on a tree.

Ciara woke from a slumber with a start, her heart racing, adrenaline pumping through her body as if she were in battle. *Brenn!* He was in trouble. That could be the only explanation for it. She felt it the moment her name fell from his lips and the shackles that kept her bound to the Clyss burst free. The binding spell had been lifted. She rose from the water and spread her wings. *Freedom. At last.* Her dragon had been trapped on land and in water for so long that when she spread her wings, she could barely rise above the water. She flapped them a few times, concentrating on lifting her huge reptilian body into the air. Brenn was in danger. He needed her now. She felt it with her heart and her soul. Determined to fulfill her destiny, to do her duty by her lifemate and guard him against all danger, she flapped her wings again. That time she rose as high as the trees but came crashing down to the ground.

Frustrated, she closed her eyes and tried to conjure up her sorceress powers, her magick, but of course, that was of no use. She could only use some simple spells. She would not regain all of her magick until she was completely released from bondage. She might be free of the valley, but she was still under Cewrick's spell.

She had to rely on her dragon. Ciara could see her mate in her mind's eye, the danger he was in. She also saw the monster about to slay and eat him. *By the goddess, this is not going to happen. My lifemate found me. I am not going to lose him to a morcoug.* If Brenn were killed, the soul shard, that precious crystal tear, would fall to Cewrick and she would be lost forever. Her soul would be gone, and with it, all hope of rescuing her people. Again she flapped her wings with fierce determination and finally rose into the sky.

Memories of watching her family fly reminded her that she was a sight to behold. Against the sunlight, her wings were almost a transparent mauve, the bones barely visible. Her purple body was a vision of silvery-mauve scales.

She soared, not even relishing the freedom of the sky or her ability to fly again. Her only thought was to go and save her lifemate.

CHAPTER FOUR

B renn's lifeblood was draining from his body. The monster's talons were as long and sharp as his sword, and they had ripped his chest open. He had not been able to inflict any damage to the creature. As rumored, the monster's skin was tougher than the side of a cliff. It was a miracle that his blade had not broken. But it was a sword passed down to him from his grandfather, the blade infused with magick. It was also fashioned from a unique and precious metal, an ore that only his pride mined. The sorcerer wanted those mines, the metal ore and the crystals they mined. What Cewrick did not know was that it was not only the metal that made their swords special, but the magick attached to them.

He lunged at the creature again and slashed at its legs, but the sword merely bounced off the hard skin. His sword would not break, Brenn knew. But even the magick of the sword could not defeat these monsters. The beast reached down to him, its claw open to capture him, but Brenn jumped to the side. Instead, the claw sent him flying, slamming him hard against the trunk of a tree.

Stunned, he lay there, the world spinning around him. He knew these were his last moments. He could feel the life leaving his body with every labored breath he took. *Oh, gods, my family.* Ivran could not save their pride on his own and did not have the connections to the king to enlist his help.

As his lifeblood drained from his body, his fogged mind drifted to his temptress from that one enchanted night. His heart ached at the thought of never encountering her again, even if she had just been a feverish hallucination. At least he would die with the beautiful vision of her on his mind. "Ciara," he whispered again as his hand clutched the pouch. The tingling ran through his fingers, up his arm, fierce now, as if lightning entered his body. It did not stop at his chest, like before. He felt it throughout every fiber of his being.

His eyes glazed, the world around him becoming a blur. A flash of violet above made him blink fiercely to clear the fog. Was that a dragon he saw up high? The monster stood close to him now, its claws ready to snatch him up, its jaw prepared to devour him, its drool almost dripping onto his chest.

A blast of hot air surrounded his body. Such intense heat. *Where did that come from?* Through the haze, he saw a stream of fire set the monster ablaze before it could grab him. Its bellow of pain almost deafened him as it retreated into the woods, its thick hide blazing and a dragon hovering above it.

Brenn opened his eyes to see Ivran sitting beside him. "Are we dead?"

Ivran smiled. "No. You would have been if it had not been for a dragon that rescued you. It saved both of us. The morcoug would have attacked me, as I was trying to divert its attention away from you."

"The dragon was not a dream?"

"No. I have never seen a dragon like it. It was purple and mauve and silver. It healed you," Ivran said.

"How?"

"Even if the morcoug did not get to kill you, your wounds would have. The beast splayed open your chest. When the dragon approached and set the beast on fire, I quickly hid again. It sat beside you, and I watched as it bent its head and allowed its tears to heal your wounds. I saw it all from my hiding place in the trees."

"A friendly magical dragon?" Brenn asked.

Ivran laughed. "I would think so. It saved us from the monster and healed you."

Brenn sat up and rubbed his chest. He felt no wounds, no scars. "I feel fine now. I do not understand any of this, but we need to continue our journey. Where is Atom?"

"Atom is fine. He is rested. Twink was a little ruffled, but he stayed safe, cushioned in that cloak of yours. You should rest, too, Brenn. You've been through quite an ordeal."

Brenn stood, feeling strangely invigorated. "No rest. We need to go on. I am actually very hungry. I could eat a harteox. You packed some of the leftover fish, did you?"

They ate the fish, drank some water, then continued on their journey. As they left the forest and began the trek across a veld, Brenn suddenly noticed a speck high in the sky. "Ivran, look up. Is that a dragon I see?"

"Yes. It is not a black dragon. It looks like the dragon that saved you. It is purple."

"By the goddess. Is it following us?"

"It would seem so."

"Such strange magick has happened these last days," Brenn said under his breath as he returned his attention to the road ahead.

His thoughts drifted to the morning at the pool, soft alabaster skin taking on a silvery, purplish-mauve sheen, flashes of light so bright he had to shield his eyes. It had happened so fast. One moment, he had held Ciara in his arms and the next, she was gone. Instead of his beautiful siren, he had seen a purple dragon slithering into the pool of water.

It was a dream, right? It has to be!

The only dragons he knew of were the black creatures that protected Cewrick's realm, and the jewel dragons in the stories his father used to tell him. He looked back up at the dragon flying high above them and smiled in wonder. Could his temptress be real? Maybe he had not been hallucinating. After all, Ivran had seen the dragon, had seen it heal his wounds. His friend had said the gaping chest wounds should have killed him. But here he was. Alive and well, his chest unmarked. No one would ever know looking at his chest that it had been splayed open, his lifeblood soaking the soil. The morcoug had been very real, and surely he and Ivran would not share the same hallucination?

There were the legends, told by his forefathers and passed down through the generations, of jewel-toned protector dragons that had filled the sky until a curse had been placed upon them. But that was all they were. Legends. No one in his lifetime had ever seen one.

He reached up and grasped the leather pouch resting on his chest. That familiar fire burst across his skin.

They reached the outskirts of Arluc as the suns were setting. The storm and morcoug attack had cost them valuable travel time.

Younglings played outside of homes built from woodbine with thatched roofs of woven nettaweed. Several played a game of chase, giggling in delight as a couple of koras happily jumped and nipped at their heels.

Women on their way home from the market that was on the other side of the village carried woven baskets filled with fruit, vegetables, and other sundries.

The village was buzzing with the activities of daily life. Nothing was amiss. That fact was not lost on Brenn. The Arlucians were a peaceful people that often traded their wares with farmers and merchants from Brenn's village. But the Arlucians were human. They were unaware of the well-kept secret—that all the occupants of Xynnar were lion shifters. They knew of the black dragons and the urcals and magick. They were aware of the evil sorcerer living in his monstrous castle and threatening them all. And they, too, knew the legends. All people on Ierilia were aware, even the cave dwellers.

Brenn slowed Atom to a walk and turned to glance at Ivran. "What say you we find a tavern for a hot meal and shelter for the night? Maybe someone saw or heard something that could help us find answers to what happened to our home."

Ivran nodded in agreement. "I find it odd that nothing seems amiss here. With this village being so close to ours, they would have seen the ships in the sky. When the attack happened, as I told you, I was on my way back after a fishing expedition. I could see the ships miles away from our village. I hurried back, but by that time the village was ablaze, and I hid in that hollow tree. Even the fires would have lit up the sky and could be seen from afar."

"What time was it, Ivran?"

"The suns had almost set."

"This village is three hours from Xynnar, and if it was not quite dark yet, the people here would not have seen anything."

"True. And the fire raged a very short time. It was a strange kind of fire. The laser beams from the ship were green in color. They incinerated everything almost instantly."

"What about our cattle? The horses?"

"They only aimed at the houses. I already told you. Our

41

animals were still in the meadow but got spooked. We'll have to hunt them down. Stop making me repeat myself."

Brenn grimaced. He had so much on his mind with what had all happened in a short period of time, like his enchantress, then to find his village destroyed and everyone missing, that everything kind of jumbled together. "Sorry. I will probably ask again," he apologized.

He stopped outside a stable used by travelers to feed and rest their horses. Many traders used these stables to house horses for sale. The shop next to it sold saddles, bridles and attachments, halters, stirrups, bits, and other basic riding supplies.

As they were dismounting Atom, a young boy of about thirteen with big blue eyes and a mop of unruly sable hair ran out to greet them. Both men looked at him in shock.

"Tomas!" Brenn engulfed the lad in a tight hug. "It is good to see you!" He let go of the youngster and looked at Ivran. He looked just as shocked as he was to see the boy and he engulfed him in a hug as well. The young one wriggled loose, apparently puzzled by such a heartfelt greeting as if they had not seen each other in many years.

Tomas' father, Laro, was a horse breeder from their village. He often traveled the valley with his son, selling some of the horses he bred, as well as handmade tack and saddles created by his cousin Kira. Laro's mate had passed on during the birth of their son, and he had never taken another.

Ivran ruffled the boy's hair as he released him from the hug. "Where's your father, sprout?"

Tomas groaned and made a comical face at him. He was short in stature, so had gained the nickname. "He's at the market getting Kira that girl smelling stuff she likes so much. He should be back shortly."

Brenn looked at Ivran, both men silently agreeing not to upset the youngster with the truth that their families were missing, that their village was gone.

"Tell your father to meet us at the Molten Eel Tavern," Brenn instructed. "Here's a coin. Go buy yourself something nice." He took a gold coin out of his money pouch and handed it to Tomas.

The lad's face lit up, and he smiled broadly. "Thanks, Brenn. That is gold. That will buy me a new blanket for my horse."

"You can earn another coin if you'll do something for me. Twinkle, my sister's pet, snuck into my saddlebag. I cannot take him along on my journey, and I do not want to ride all the way back. Do you think you can take care of him for me until we return?" Brenn asked.

Tomas nodded. "Sure can. But we are going home in a few days. I can give him to Shanina."

Brenn did not answer. Time enough after they told Laro about the abduction of their people and what had happened to their village. Laro would know how to break it to his son. He took Twinkle out of his saddlebag and handed him to Tomas. Twinkle protested, but then he cuddled against Tomas' neck and settled on his shoulder.

Brenn and Ivran chuckled as Tomas took off like an arrow, clutching his prize tightly in one hand and holding Twinkle with the other so he would not fall off his shoulder.

They entered the stables. Brenn paid the stable hand handsomely to look after Atom and also asked if the lad could take Atom to the blacksmith to check his shoes. Through a back door, they accessed the corral that held the horses that were for sale. "Take your pick," Brenn told Ivran. "Make sure to pick a strong horse. We have a long journey ahead of us."

Ivran chose a copper-colored stallion. They led the horse into the stable, and Brenn gave the stable hand more coin to look after the horse. "You'll have to give him a name," he told Ivran as they went to the adjoining shop to buy horse gear and to pay for the horse.

Ivran nodded. "When I patted his nose, I saw a sparkle in his eyes. We bonded immediately. His name will be Sparks."

"Good choice. Go choose your horse gear, and do not be shy about prices. I told you, I have enough gold coin with me to buy ten or more horses and then some. After you are done, we'll get a room at the tavern, eat, and wait for Laro. The suns have almost set. The market will be closing soon."

Brenn paid the tavern keeper for a room, then ordered a meal for them both. He knew the tavern keeper and his chosen mate quite well.

"Brenn! Are you home for a spell?" Tarn, the tavern keeper, asked and slapped Brenn on the shoulder.

"Yes. The war is over, and I am home for several moons. How is Garata? The last time I saw you, she was expecting to give birth."

Tarn smiled from ear to ear. "We had a girl."

"My congratulations. She will be spoiled by her four big brothers. Ivran and I would like a hearty meal and a pint of cosmic mead for each of us. Oh, and we are expecting Laro to join us. Same for him when he arrives."

"Garata cooked up a large cauldron of korobeast stew. The marketers have marked down all their wares, and a lot of travelers are passing through. It has been very busy," Tarn said.

Brenn looked at all the customers sitting or standing and nodded. "I see that. Good for business, huh?"

"With the festival season in full swing, I expect it to get even busier," Tarn agreed.

Brenn and Ivran sat at a little table near a window. "Quaint village. I always like coming here. Their market is fantastic. So many traders from all over Ierilia sell their wares there. It opens very early, at sunrise. We'll go there to buy you a bedroll, and we need to buy more blankets. You will need weapons, too."

Tarn returned with two large bowls of steaming stew, a platter of freshly baked bread, and a pitcher of mead

"I know your tavern is usually full of people from all over the valley. Have you heard any talk of strange happenings, like ship sightings?" Brenn asked as Tarn placed the food and mead on the table.

"I've heard nothing of ships, but I have overheard several people mention sighting a purple dragon this evening," Tarn replied, shaking his head. "I think they drank too much eldalas spirit."

"Thanks, Tarn. The food smells delicious," Brenn said, not responding to the mention of a purple dragon. "Put it on my bill. I will pay you before I leave tomorrow."

They were halfway through their meal when Laro joined them.

"Brenn, you are back from battle! I presume you were victorious. Ivran, what brings you here?" Laro pulled up a chair and joined them. "Are you staying the night in the tavern?"

"Yes, we are. Where is Tomas?" Ivran said.

"We are lodging with a friend. Tomas has already gone to their house. You were very generous giving my boy a gold coin, Brenn. Too much for a young lad."

"I need him to take care of Twinkle for me. Laro, we have some terrible news." Brenn lowered his voice so nearby people could not hear him. He told Laro about their village, their missing families and friends.

"Do you think they were killed? Incinerated?" Laro's hand shook as he picked up his pint of cosmic mead and took several swallows.

"Ssh, keep your voice down. No one knows. I do not think they are dead. I looked thoroughly through the charred debris and saw no evidence that people were burned. They were taken, but we do not know why or for what purpose. Ivran and I are on our way to see King Biryn to inform him of it. This is a battle we cannot wage on horseback."

"I am going with you," Laro told them. "Tomas can stay here."

Brenn nodded in agreement. "Good. I will pay for Tomas' lodging. We will need an army and the king's fleet to defeat the Toubosians. King Biryn will have insight. Do not tell anyone. We do not want to start a widespread panic. Meet us at sunrise at the market. We'll need to buy supplies for several days of riding."

They ate in silence for a little while until they had finished the stew and bread. Laro rubbed his belly. "Thank you. That was good. Hey, did you hear about the purple dragon? A lot of people have seen it. It seems the legends we've heard for so many years are true."

Ivran and Brenn glanced at each other. "Yes, we saw it high up above. It seems friendly," Brenn said.

"But we do not not really know, do we?" Laro commented.

"The legends say the jewel-toned dragons were protectors. I do not think we need to fear it," Ivran said.

Laro stood. "Thank you again for the meal. I will bed down for the night. It has been a long day. I will see you both at sunrise at the market."

"I think we should head for our room, too," Brenn suggested. "We need a good night's rest before we head out tomorrow."

CHAPTER FIVE

Both men were well rested and awake before sunrise. After eating their modest meal of crusty bread and jago milk cheese, they washed up at the pump outside and returned to the bar to pay for their lodging and meal.

Tarn said, "Garata put together a few things for you for your journey. It is nothing much, just some bread, dried fruit, and cheese. She also packed some of those hirthseed cakes you like so much and a wineskin of cosmic mead." He pushed a wrapped package and a wineskin toward Brenn.

Brenn grinned as he gave him a couple of gold coins in return. "She makes the best hirthseed cakes. Please thank her for me."

Tarn gaped at Brenn. "This is too much!" he exclaimed as he tried to give one of the coins back to Brenn.

"No, please keep it. Garata's package is worth the coin to me."

"She will be glad to know her cooking is so valued. Have a safe journey, my friend."

Brenn and Ivran took their leave of Tarn and headed out into the village streets.

Ivran glanced at Brenn as they made their way to the

market. "Tarn and Garata treat you almost as if you were their youngling."

Brenn looked at his friend. "I was on my way back to the capital after my last furlough and found Garata's older brother trapped under an overturned cart on the road to our village. Something had spooked his horse. If I had not come along when I did, he would have perished."

They made their way to where Laro was waiting at the market. Tomas was standing with his father, cuddling Twinkle and petting its soft fur. The little antuar seemed to be warming up to the boy very quickly. Laro had several bundles of goods by his feet. He was holding a leather-wrapped package that had the hilts of a couple of swords peeking out of it, and he had a bedroll under his arm.

"Laro," Brenn called to get his attention.

Laro turned and grinned at both Brenn and Ivran. "While you slept in this morning, I've managed to acquire the supplies we need for our journey," he said as he tossed a bedroll to Ivran.

Brenn shook his head at Laro in surprise. "The suns are barely over the horizon. How did you manage to get this so early?"

"My friend Kolin trades camping supplies. He has been eyeing one of Kira's saddles for quite some time. I managed to haggle with him for the supplies as well as travel cakes, dried meat, and fruit-bread his mate makes. Tomas will be staying with his family during our trip. He'll earn his keep by working for Kolin."

"And the swords?" Ivran asked.

"The blacksmith was on the way to the market."

Brenn clapped both men on the shoulder. "Come, we must make haste. With Atom well rested, we should be able to make it to Inar Ridge before sunset."

Laro turned to Tomas, a look of sadness crossing his face.

He ruffled the boy's hair. "I'm not sure how long I will be away, but you be sure to help Kolin with his wares and animals." Brenn knew Laro had sold horses from Kolin's herd during their stops at different villages throughout the valley.

"I will, Father," Tomas said as they hugged each other goodbye.

The men gathered their supplies and made their way to the stables.

"I'm going to buy a packhorse," Brenn decided. "We have too much for our horses to carry."

While Ivran and Laro saddled the horses, Brenn haggled with the trader.

"Where are the three of you going?" Bluko, the owner of the stables, asked.

"Hunting. I am on leave from army duties for several moons, and Ivran is taking some time away from his shop with the permission of his mate. Laro only has Tomas who will stay with friends while we are gone. We have not seen each other in a long time." Brenn did not waste too much time haggling with the trader. They still needed to go to the market before commencing their journey. Tarn and Garata had given them enough food for the ride to Xynnar, but it would not suffice for the journey ahead. Time was of the essence. After countering twice, he settled. "Sold. I will take the stallion, the gray abascos."

An abascos was a breed only found in the Xararian Mountains. A very big, sturdy, six-legged horse, it could carry a heavy load and still move swiftly.

"Okay. Your name is Storm. Hear me?" He patted the horse on its nose. "With your dark gray mane and dark and light gray fur, you remind me of the storm we just passed through on our way here."

The horse's ears perked as if he understood. "Good boy, Storm. We have got quite an adventure ahead. I hope you are up for it." He quickly joined his friends. "We have a packhorse. I have also bought gear for him. Here's the stable hand with him now."

"He looks like he'll last the journey," Ivran commented.

"Yes. That is why I bought him. His name is Storm. We need to buy more supplies before we head out. Let's finish packing our gear and hit the market."

They found the market already bustling when they got there. Brenn purchased more non-perishable food and another wineskin and dried fruits. "Stop," he said suddenly. "It is a good plan to purchase medicinal herbs and spices and bandages. Just in case."

He halted them at the herbalist's stand. "Joveh, I need traveling supplies, in case one of us is attacked during our hunt. There are three of us," he told the trader.

Joveh put together a kit for him. "It is wise to take such supplies, Brenn. Where are you going to hunt?"

"Near the Avago plains. I heard there was a large herd of harteox in the area."

Satisfied they had everything they needed, the trio headed out of the village. Brenn hoped and prayed to the gods and goddesses their journey would be uneventful. But one never knew. Just the thought of the morcoug that had attacked him and Ivran drove that point home. He shivered at the memory of the beast and the damage it had done to his chest. If it had not been for the dragon…

His mind drifted back to the purple dragon, and he glanced at the sky. Far up above, he saw a tiny speck. Was it a bird? Could it be the dragon? Absentmindedly, he reached for the pouch and grasped it. Sharp bolts of lightning shot through his shoulder, down his arm to his elbow and to his hand. His skin prickled. Within seconds, he heard the flapping of wings. He looked up and saw her in all her magnificence. He gasped. He had never seen such beauty.

"Brenn! Look up!" Ivran shouted.

The horses reared, then settled. "So, it is true, then? The legend?" Laro asked.

Brenn nodded. "It seems so. I am glad I am not the only one witnessing this now. I was afraid I was inflicted with a disease of the brain."

Ivran scolded him. "I already told you the dragon healed you. Do you think I would lie to you? You should have been dead."

The dragon swooped upward but circled above them until they continued.

"So what happened, Brenn? It appears you did not tell me everything," Laro said as they pushed onward.

"A morcoug attacked us. I fought it," Brenn answered, then told him the story. Ivran continued with his side of the tale.

Laro whistled. "The gods and goddesses smiled upon you, friend. No one survives such an attack."

"Enough about me. What did you tell your son where we are going, Laro?" Brenn asked.

"Exactly what you told the traders. We are hunting. That you wanted to bring home meat. Tomas was very surprised because I normally do not hunt. I buy our food at the market. I told him I needed a respite from everyday routine, that I was tired of always traveling and working. His thought was that maybe I'm looking for a new mate, but he wished me good luck."

"Well, you never know, Laro. Maybe you'll find your lifemate during our travels." Ivran chuckled.

"It is true. I have been alone since Tomas was born and not touched another woman. Even though Khrissa was not my true lifemate, I loved her with all my heart. But I am weary of loneliness. I'm still young."

"We all have a lifemate, Laro. I admire you for not touching any other women. The tavern wenches can give you an incurable disease. As you know, they sleep with anyone willing to pay. I am sure you will find your lifemate as sure as I am I will find mine," Brenn said.

"We are all wondering why you are still alone, Brenn," Laro glanced at Brenn.

"I've been waiting for the right woman." Brenn rode ahead, not wanting to continue the conversation. He had already met his lifemate. He knew that. Ciara. But he still felt unsure, and he could not share it with his friends.

CHAPTER SIX

After riding for a full uneventful day, they made camp near a gurgling stream. Rather than eat their dried meats and fish, they waded into the stream and caught some fresh fish. They roasted them on guzona leaves over the fire while they squatted around it and talked about old times. They avoided the subject of their heartrending knowledge about their destroyed village and the disappearance of loved ones and friends. They ate the fresh bread and some dried fruits, then, after drinking some mead, relaxed on their spread-out bedrolls.

Brenn felt his eyelids drooping when he suddenly heard rustling in the bushes. One of the horses whinnied. Instantly wide awake, he sat up and looked at his companions. Both were almost asleep. Something was not right. His journey home had been rife with danger—the worst was his battle with the dryons before he made it to the Clyss Valley. He pictured them in his mind for a moment. Once, centuries ago, the dryons had been lion shifters. Brenn's pride was the only lion shifting pride on the planet, so it was possible they were his ancestors that had been captured by Cewrick and stripped of their humanity. He wondered if he would look like them if he were able to shift into his lion. They were large, fierce, essentially majestic-looking beasts. Instead of fur, their huge, lion-shaped bodies were covered in metallic golden scales, almost as if they wore plated armor. The color of the scales could change to blend in with their surroundings. What should have been a mane became armored quills that framed their heads in a more in-depth gold mixed with brown. The dryons that had attacked him were males, as the females had no mane and were slightly smaller.

So many creatures that otherwise keep away from humans have been moving closer to villages and roads, preying on unsuspecting children and women and travelers for food. What is the cause of this?

He could not dwell on these thoughts as he heard another sound.

"Ivran," he said very softly and poked him. Then he shook Laro's arm. "Sssh, there's something in the bushes."

"I hear it," Ivran whispered.

"Something or someone is watching us."

"What do we do?" Laro asked.

"We wait. Have your sword ready," Brenn hissed.

Suddenly, glowing yellow eyes glared at them from the surrounding brush. Brenn, Ivran, and Laro sat back to back, their swords ready, on the alert to jump up and battle whatever it was that was stalking them.

They heard a loud growl. The yellow eyes grew bigger, and the predator emerged from the bushes. It was a quartz lion. Brenn knew it was not alone. More than ever, he ached to shift into his lion. His lion could best the beast, but that was not an option open to him. Could they fight the animals as humans? They were only three, and Laro and Ivran were not experienced warriors, but Brenn had seen more than one pair of glowing yellow eyes. These were real lions, the beasts having no human instinct whatsoever. And they were big, their claws sharp and long, their teeth vicious and like daggers. One bite in the neck could kill the fiercest of warriors.

"By the gods, we are done for," Laro hissed.

"I don not understand. I traveled this path many times and encountered nothing. Why is all this happening now?" Brenn murmured loud enough for his friends to hear.

"The sorcerer. Cewrick. There is no other explanation," Laro answered.

Ivran joined in. "I agree. All of us have traveled these trails safely. Suddenly we are attacked by predators? It does not make any sense."

The lion crept slowly toward them. Brenn kept an eye on the other glowing eyes, but so far, only one of the lions approached them. The beast opened its mouth. Brenn shuddered at the elongated teeth, at the foul breath that wafted toward him. Did he really want to fight this animal? Surely, somewhere in the distant past, his pride must have been related to the beasts. Then again, why would Cewrick have created two species of lions, the dryons, and the quartz lions? Maybe the quartz lions were a true species, but he could not remember an attack from them. Ever. The quartz lions had always kept to their territory. They had never attacked a human. It had to be Cewrick's doing. There was no other answer.

The beast was so close he could almost touch its head. Brenn leaned back. It opened its mouth and roared. A dozen or more lions jumped out of the bushes.

"Ye gods," Brenn uttered. His hand clasped the pouch for a moment. "Ciara, if you are real, I really need you now."

He jumped out of the brush, his sword ready, and from the corner of his eye, he saw Ivran and Laro do the same. The lion lifted its colossal paw, talons extended. Brenn drew in his breath. If that paw hit him, that would be the end. He raised his sword above his head and swung, cutting the lion's foot clean off. The lion roared in pain and anger. It did not stop him from attacking. On three legs, it advanced again. Vaguely

Brenn wondered how his friends were faring. Could they defend themselves against the giant lions?

The lion reared, its intact claw ready to strike Brenn. He held his sword ready above his head, swinging it around in a circle, ready to strike. Heat. The same kind he had felt before. Within a second, the lion incinerated into ashes. Fire flashed from above. Several of the other lions fell to the fire. The others fled.

Brenn lowered his sword and rested it on the ground. He looked up and saw her, the purple dragon. Her long tongue flicked in and out, her mouth wide open as she breathed fire upon his attackers. She was beyond beautiful with her glowing scales. Her eyes were ablaze with a purple hue as she gazed down at him.

"Ciara," he whispered. "It is really true."

I love you, my warrior. I am your guardian. Your lifemate. But until the spell is lifted, I am trapped as my dragon.

Had he really heard those words? The dragon disappeared. The air was rife with the stench of burned fur and lion flesh. Brenn sank down and looked behind him. Ivran and Laro were not hurt, but they were stunned.

They returned to their campsite and Brenn stoked the fire, then threw some fresh branches on it. Within seconds, flames licked the dry wood. They crouched close to the fire, Laro handing the wineskin around.

"Did all that really happen?" Laro asked.

"It did, but it has to remain a secret between us," Brenn said.

"How did you get to have a jewel dragon as a guardian?" Laro demanded to know.

"She is my lifemate."

"Nonsense. You are a lion shifter. How can you mate with a dragon? That is impossible," Laro said.

"She is a shifter, but she's bound."

"She still cannot be your mate. Never has anyone in history

mated with a foreign shifter. It is unheard of." Laro rubbed his chin.

"I know. It is a first. But I know it for a fact. She is my lifemate, even if she is a dragon shifter. I cannot explain it. I just know it to be true."

"How can you ever be together? Have offspring?" Laro asked.

Ivran turned toward Laro. "Does it all really matter? She saved us from annihilation. Right now, I do not care about old laws, traditions, and whatever else. The purple dragon is guarding us."

"We have a long day's journey ahead of us tomorrow. We should get some sleep with what little time we have left of this night," Brenn said as he relaxed on his bedroll. Ivran and Laro followed his lead.

Brenn was restless, on the alert for any sound from the surrounding brush and trees. Sometimes something caused him to sit upright. Several times he even jumped up to scout around, and he heard Laro and Ivran do the same. The lion attack had scared the wits out of them. The fact that Ciara had to save his life twice brought home that because of the curse, he was not whole. He was half the warrior he should be. How could he be the lifemate she needed him to be if he could not keep himself or his friends safe?

The quartz lions did not have a sprinkle of humanity. The dragon attack probably hardly phased any remaining beasts. They could still be lurking, watching the humans, and attack again after they succumbed to sleep. *One of us should have kept watch for a few hours, each of us taking turns. At least we would get some rest. Tomorrow night we'll need to do that, because what if Ciara is not near enough to help?*

Between his worry about the lions, his mind was constantly on the beautiful creature that had so far saved his life twice. Even as a dragon, she was utterly mesmerizing. Her jewel-toned scales reminded him of the fire opals his sister loved so much. He remembered the silky feel of Ciara's iridescent scales as he had traced his fingers across her skin just a few nights before. So much had happened since then. Closing his hand around the leather pouch, he whispered Ciara's name.

That familiar tingling heat infused his body. He did not fight it. The intense, pleasurable warmth reminded him of her silken touch. A soft glow engulfed his body, and he suddenly could feel a form materializing within his arms.

"Ciara!" He gasped as her human body solidified in his arms. "How can this be?"

"Shhh." Her luminous eyes met his as she ran her fingertips from his jawline to his muscular neck, down his arm, to close around his hand that still grasped the leather pouch that held her soul shard. "I only have my human body until the suns rise. Let us not lose a moment with talk of things neither of us can resolve just yet."

Brenn wasted no time as he stood and held his hand out for her to take. Pulling her to her feet and into his arms, he held her, then leaned down to place a tender kiss on her lips. "Come, let us find someplace more private." He grabbed his bedroll and led her a slight distance from the camp, far enough for their privacy but close enough to Ivran and Laro to assist them should they fall under attack again.

He spread his bedroll beneath the boughs of a young yewnettle tree, the tree trunk large enough to keep them hidden from view of the campsite. Seating himself on his bedroll with his back against the trunk, he pulled Ciara onto his lap and captured her mouth in a scorching kiss. Her hands pulled at his belt, his codpiece, releasing his throbbing erection.

Her arms snaked around his neck as she met his kiss with a passion that seared his soul. Brenn lifted his head to drink in the exquisite beauty of her. He ran his thumb over her swollen lips, down her silvery neck to the scales between her breasts, to the pearly nipple of her left breast.

"Gods, I burn for you. From the moment you beckoned me in the waters of the Clyss, you captured not only my heart but my soul as well." Brenn's gaze moved back up to her beautiful eyes, drowning in the deep purple of her passion as he continued to stroke her nipple. She gasped as he leaned his head down to capture that taut nipple into his mouth, teasing it with little nips and kisses, then suckling it while his fingers tweaked her other nipple and he massaged her breast.

"Brenn," Ciara moaned, "by the goddess, please, I need to touch and taste you, too." She shifted to straddle him, sliding her moist folds back and forth against his engorged cock.

Suddenly she swung around, slipping her body up his chest until her pussy touched his chin. He sucked in his breath as he felt her long hair stroke his thighs, as her lips tantalized the slit of his cock. He was bursting to come. Her hand fondled his taut sack, her fingers teasing the spot between sack and cock. He bucked, trying to enter her mouth.

There was a rustling in the surrounding brush, causing the fire within him to douse immediately. He grasped her, only to hold a changing body. She rolled off him. Within seconds, her dragon emerged.

Bewildered, Brenn gazed up at the beautiful reptile. She looked down at him for a moment, then flapped her silken wings and rose upward.

His guardian. She had sensed the danger, too, and had reacted. He quickly put on his codpiece and belt and returned to camp. Laro and Ivran slept soundly, both snoring. The fire had died down to embers. Brenn threw more wood on the fire, and after placing his bedroll close to it, he lay down, staring at the flames. He could sleep in peace now in the knowledge that Ciara was watching over them, that whatever was lurking in the bushes would be fearful enough of the dragon.

CHAPTER SEVEN

All three were awake and up at sunrise. "I guess your guardian kept watch over us last night," Ivran commented as he roasted a rukan bird over the fire. "Everything was quiet."

The aroma caused Brenn's stomach to growl. "I suppose it was," he answered. *If only they knew.*

"If we don not encounter any delays, we should reach Troncania by sundown," Laro said, accepting a chunk of rukan from Ivran.

Brenn took a few bites of the tasty meat. He nodded. "Yes. We need to stock up on bread and mead, and our wineskin is near empty."

While he ate, he thought for a moment about Ciara. Their interlude had been so abruptly interrupted. He now knew that she was real. It was not his imagination or a hallucination brought on by his innermost wishes and the magic of the bottomless basin. But like his friends, he wondered how it was possible. How could a lion shifter mate with a dragon shifter, one that was supposed to be extinct? Most of it was still beyond his comprehension, but at least he knew that Ciara was watching over him and his friends, that she was his lifemate, the woman with whom he would spend eternity.

What had she told him? She was bound to her dragon. Had Cewrick placed a curse on her, just like the sorcerer had on his pride? The legends of the jewel dragons had been told for years, the tales of the beautiful dragons passed on through the generations. When he was a boy, they were great bedtime stories. All he had ever known were the black dragons that attacked villages, and at times, abducted people. They were Cewrick's minions.

"Brenn!" Ivran yelled.

Brenn startled. "What's wrong?"

"Nothing. You are staring at the sky and not saying anything," Laro said.

"Sorry. I was thinking," Brenn excused. "Thank you, Laro, for catching this bird and plucking it for breakfast. Nice change from fish."

"You can hunt for tomorrow's breakfast or lunch. Let's pack up and get moving," Laro grumbled.

They packed their gear, saddled the horses, and took the well-ridden trail to Troncania.

Located near the base of Inar Ridge, the Troncanians were known for mining fire opals and irorcan ore used to fuel ships and other technological devices abundant in the capital and other villages and towns beyond the Inar Ridge. It was said that irorcan ore, when combined with the koriam crystals mined in the mountains near Xynnar and used to make weapons, could create a weapon so powerful it could destroy whole villages and towns, maybe even a planet. So far none of their scientists that he knew of had been able to combine the two substances without the compound becoming unstable.

Brenn looked up and saw Ciara flying lower in the sky than she had previously. Her violet scales flashed in the suns' light as she scouted ahead and back to ensure their path remained clear of any predators that could attack.

With her keeping the way clear, they reached Troncania well before the suns set. But what should have been a bustling village was silent. There was no laughter from children playing in the streets, no women going about their daily activities, no smoke wafting from chimneys. There was nothing. The village appeared to be completely abandoned.

Brenn watched as Ciara flew the length of the village and back, feeling the familiar brush of her mind in his.

I see nothing, no villagers or animals. The market is abandoned, the tables are still full of goods to be sold. I see no predators. It is safe for you and your friends. Her sweet voice resonated in his mind. He wished she would message him more, but maybe it was difficult from up high.

"It appears the Troncanians have vanished, just like our people. At least their village was left intact," Brenn said as he reined in Atom at the stables and dismounted. "Let us rest the horses here and explore the village on foot. I think the disappearance of our pride and the destruction of our village are related to what may have happened to the Troncanians."

Laro looked at Brenn as he and Ivran dismounted their horses. "I agree with your suspicions. I was in this village about a month ago trading for fire opals to bring back home to Xynnar."

Their pride had no interest in trading for irorcan ore, preferring to use ironde ore combined with the koriam crystals to smelt the metal used in their weapons. Their smelting process stabilized the koriam, allowing them to carry their weapons out of the valley without incident. His pride would give their lives to keep that secret. No one dared to remove the koriam from the valley for fear of destroying the cities beyond.

Much of the technological equipment used by many beyond the Inar Ridge reacted to the koriam crystals in their valley. Many of the devices simply stopped working, but recently, a ship that had landed on the mountain where their people mined the crystals exploded, killing the members of the crew within it and wounding many of the Laeturians meeting them to trade.

The closer those travel devices were brought to the mountain range leading into the Clyss Valley, the more unstable their technology became. The Troncanians were the only people on the west side of the ridge that had any type of technology, but it was limited to the mining equipment they used along the mountain ridge where they mined their irorcan ore.

"We'll tether the horses and explore separately. We should be able to make it to the market and back here before nightfall," Brenn said as they tied the horses' reins to the hitching post. Grabbing their weapons, the men fanned out to explore the deserted village.

Brenn entered the inn, his sword drawn, his senses on alert. Ciara might be guarding them against outside threats, but within the walls of the building and cottages, she could not help. The stench of rotting food overwhelmed him. He glanced around and saw half-eaten bowls of stew and platters of bread, cheese, and fruit on the tables, along with glasses and pitchers of mead. Some were still full as if the innkeeper had just placed them on the table. Small packs, leather coin pouches, and purses had fallen to the floor or lay on empty chairs, the coins and belongings abandoned by their owners.

Brenn made his way to the bar, then the stairs leading to the rooms above. Quickly and quietly, he reached the top of the stairs and entered the first room he came to. Abandoned. It was the same for each room he checked. All belongings had been left behind and no person was to be seen.

Going back down the stairs, he walked into the kitchens and the storeroom. He gathered together several filled wineskins, a wheel of cheese, and some dried meat. He was about to leave some coin for the owners but decided to compensate the innkeeper in the future. Looting was possible and gold coin would disappear fast. *Is that not what I am doing? Well, this is an emergency. I am sure Jazzug will understand.* He placed the spoils into an empty flour sack and carried it with him, leaving the sack outside the door of the inn as he continued his exploration of the village.

Toys lay abandoned in front of homes. Some doors stood open, as if whoever lived in the homes had tried to flee. Brenn wondered if it was any use exploring beyond the village. Were the farms abandoned, too? They could check as they continued their journey. Remaining in the village was not an option. They would camp in the next forest. With Ciara guarding them, it should be safe enough.

He came to the last house, glanced at it, and was about to turn around and head back to the stables when he heard a sound. He stopped, sword drawn and ready. The door was ajar. He kicked it wide open and carefully stepped into the house. Again, the stench of rotting food entered his nostrils. A table was set, a pot of spoiled stew in the center. A loaf of bread, now green and gray, lay beside it. A dish of rancid butoro, a platter of rotting fruit, and glasses filled with curdled jago milk completed the picture. A swarm of quagga buzzed around the food. There were five place settings. The family that lived there had been ready to sit down for their meal.

Again, a soft mewling sound drifted to his ears from above. He headed for the stairs and ran up them to check the bedrooms. In what looked to be the main bedroom stood a basket on the floor filled with dirty clothing. Some of it moved. Brenn grunted. It was probably an antuar or another pet.

Gingerly, he shifted some of the smelly clothing aside. Facing him was an infant. It looked to be about two months old. He realized the smell came from the infant, its swaddling soaked and soiled. The baby cried softly. He had no idea how long ago the disaster in the village had happened. Judging by the rotting food, at least five days. It was a miracle the infant had not starved to death.

Grimacing, he crouched and removed the swaddling. He tried to cleanse the infant with some of the dirty clothes. He stood and looked around. There should be clean swaddling somewhere. Hastily exploring the other bedrooms, he found what he needed, along with a jug of water and a bowl. He awkwardly cleansed the baby, then swaddled her. It was a little girl he discovered while cleansing her. After wrapping her in a blanket he had found, he picked her up, then grabbed some extra swaddling cloths and went downstairs. Laro or Ivran would know what to do. The infant needed milk. And how could they continue their journey with an infant to care for?

Brenn hurried back to the stables, the baby now quiet. He was worried that she had succumbed to malnutrition, but when he arrived at the stables, she stirred. Laro and Ivran were already waiting for him.

"What is that?" Laro asked.

Brenn carefully flipped the blanket back, exposing the infant's face. "A newborn baby girl. She is starving. It is a miracle she is still alive. What do we do? All the food in this village has gone bad."

Laro took the infant from Brenn's arms. "She needs to suckle. We need jago milk. If she does not eat soon, she will die."

"And where do you propose we find jago milk?" Ivran asked.

"I'm sure the jagos weren not abducted. We need to ride out of here. We'll stop at one of the farms on the outskirts of the village."

Ivran laughed. "And you know how to obtain milk from a jago?"

"I do," Laro informed them. "Let's go."

"Let me go and get the sack of provisions I found at the inn," Brenn said and hurried to fetch his loot.

When he returned, his friends were already mounted and waiting. He swiftly tied the sack on their packhorse and mounted Atom. Side by side they rode out of the village.

"I see a farm," Ivran said, pointing at a house in the distance. It was surrounded by orchards and fields of vegetables. Several jagos were grazing in a meadow nearby.

"We'll see if the farm is abandoned first," Brenn said.

Spurring their horses on, they galloped to the farmhouse, but like the village, it seemed deserted. Brenn walked Atom to a large building, then dismounted and went inside. As he had suspected, it was where the farmer and his stable hands milked the jagos. There was also a large cooling room in the corner. He went to it and opened the heavy door. No farmer that supplied milk to a village would be without a cooling room. Sure enough, he saw several large containers filled with jago milk. There were also several milkskins. He filled two of them and hurried back to his friends.

"I found the farmer's milking shed and cooler. I have milk," he shouted joyfully, holding the two skins up.

"First, we have to feed the infant," Laro said. Cradling the baby, he got off his horse.

"How?" Brenn asked.

"Farmers cover their hands when milking the jago because their nipples are spiked. They will probably keep the gloves in the milking shed. We need such a glove."

Brenn hurried back to the shed. He found them on a shelf. Quickly returning to his friends, he handed them to Laro.

Laro filled a glove with milk, then cut a tip off one of the fingers. He held the dripping glove over the baby's mouth.

Brenn was amazed at Laro's ingenuity. "Where did you learn that?"

"I read it in a story," Laro said and smiled. "Look at her. Poor little thing. She was starved."

"She might not survive, even if you feed her the milk. She is so weak she can barely swallow," Ivran commented.

Brenn heard the melodic sound of Ciara's voice brush his mind. *Let me help her. I cannot use most of my magick, but as a dragon, I can still heal the little one.*

Just then, they heard the swishing sound of wings. The trees rustled as the dragon landed beside the trio. Her long neck bent, her head approached the baby. Laro began to step back, looking ready to run, but Brenn stopped him.

Brenn gazed at the beautiful dragon as a large mauve tear fell from her eye, soaking the baby's face and blanket. *Thank you for helping her.*

Ciara raised her head, looked at him, then dipped her head again to nuzzle Brenn's neck. Stepping back, she flapped her wings and soared upward.

"She has just healed the infant," Brenn told Laro and Ivran as they stared at him in shocked amazement.

Sure enough, the baby suckled the finger of the glove greedily until it was empty.

"How can we continue our journey with an infant to care for?" Ivran demanded, his pain-filled gaze on the baby.

"Ivran, surely not all the villages on our route have been raided? We'll find someone to care for her. Until then, we will have to manage," Brenn said.

Brenn looked intently at Ivran as he reached his hand up to squeeze his shoulder. "With the help of our king, we *will* find them, and we will save them. And we *will* destroy those that dared to take them!"

Ivran met Brenn's eyes and nodded his agreement. "They are my heart and soul, Brenn. I cannot bear the thought of my family injured and hurting while I am hale and whole."

The infant cooed and wiggled in Laro's arms, then started whining. A bewildered look crossed Laro's face. "Ahhhh... Thank you, little one, for the reminder that you need to be changed," he exclaimed as he held the child away from his chest.

Brenn and Ivran burst out laughing as they realized the baby had wet herself, soaking the blankets she was swaddled in.

"Let's find some more blankets. There must be some inside the farmhouse," Laro muttered, still holding her away from his chest as he made his way to the farmhouse door.

"We should make camp for the night. It is almost sundown. We could stay here. What do you think? I'm sure the farmer will not mind." Ivran laughed heartily at Laro's discomfort. "I have been in the same predicament as you with my daughter many times."

"Tomas is thirteen. It has been many years."

Brenn thought about their predicament. "It is a good plan to stay here for the night. Our horses can graze, and we'll get a comfortable night's rest. The next town is on the other side of the mountains. It is going to be difficult traveling with an infant. But it has to be. We cannot abandon her."

"I will take the horses to the corral." Ivran took the reins of all four horses.

"Wait, let me take the milkskins to the cooling room." Brenn ran after Ivran to fetch the skins.

After entering the farmhouse, they discovered that the farmer liked technology. He had a special cooling device in his kitchen and a sun-powered cooker. Brenn opened the door to the cooler and exclaimed, "Fresh food!"

"And feeding tubes for the baby," Laro said, peeking around Brenn, still holding the wet infant in his arms. "And she needs cleansing and changing."

"Yes, the tubes are already filled." Brenn felt sadness cloud his heart for the farmer and his family. "We must be sure to leave the home in clean condition. I'm confident that all these missing people are alive somewhere." *They have to be!* He knew his instincts could not be wrong, for any thought otherwise would mean that his pride, his father, mother, and sister, were all dead.

Ivran helped himself to some bread and halco slices from the cooler. He slapped the meat between two thick slices of bread. "You know something, so many generations before us, it was decided we would live off the land, that we would not embrace technology and remain a simple village, living exactly as our forefathers. But I am starting to question the sanity of that. What is wrong with a sun-powered cooler? A cooker? Is it law that we cook over open fires? That we try and preserve our food in deep cellars? What would the alpha say if I bought such items?"

"Many of the villages around ours live the old way, like to follow the old traditions. I believe the leaders of all villages and towns on this side of the mountain ridge got together and decided the same. I do not know for what reason," Brenn said while spreading his bread with butoro before adding a slice of halco. "This tastes good. I wonder if the farmer has a smoking station and he made it himself."

The baby began to cry. Clearly healed, she produced a lusty howl, telling them she was hungry. Laro quickly turned on the cooker and placed a pot filled with water on it, then fetched a feeding tube from the cooler and set it inside the pot. "Warm milk is better for her. It has been a long time since raising Tomas, but I have not forgotten."

Brenn moved toward the door. "I am going to fetch my bedroll. I do not feel comfortable sleeping in their beds. I will also fetch our wineskins. I noticed the farmer has several barrels of wine. We can refill them before we continue tomorrow."

"Can you bring mine back with you?" Ivran asked.

"Mine, too?" Laro echoed.

While Brenn went to fetch their bedrolls and wineskins, he looked up at the sky and wondered where Ciara was. Maybe she was resting in the nearby forest, he decided.

He hurried back with their bedding and wineskins and found Ivran and Laro bathing the baby in the kitchen sink. The farmer had made life even easier by installing a water pump in his kitchen that provided both hot and cold water.

"I found a small basket with infant swaddling and clothing in the living area. It is enough for a couple of changes, but we will need more," Ivran said as he glanced back down at the baby. "Look at her. She's such a pretty baby girl."

The Troncanians were a beautiful people, with copper hair and caramel skin. The infant had the traditional look and coloring of her people, but on her, everything seemed to be emphasized. Her eyes were the palest shade of blue that made the irises appear almost transparent with rings of black around them. Her slit pupils were framed by what looked like yellow fire blazing around them. She had the cutest spikes running from the tip of her little button nose, fanning above both eyebrows and coming to a V on her forehead. Her skin was a rich caramel, and the tips of her tiny, pointed ears peeked through a mass of copper ringlets that glowed like fire with gold highlights.

"We're going to have to call her something. We cannot keep calling her the infant or the baby," Laro said as he lifted her out of the bathwater and wrapped her in a soft blanket to dry her skin and handed her to Brenn.

Brenn took the infant from Laro and dressed her in clean swaddling. "What about Shuri?"

"I like Shuri," Laro said as he started cleaning the empty feeding tubes and filling them with fresh jago milk. Then he washed his shirt and the soiled swaddling he had removed from the infant earlier.

"Shuri it is," Ivran said, reaching down to tickle the baby under her chin, bringing a huge, dimpled smile to her face while her little legs kicked in delight. "I'm going to look around and see if I can find a sleeping basket and more clean clothing for her. We're going to need them to travel with her." Smiling sadly, he turned to go on his search.

Brenn lifted Shuri into his arms to cradle her after wrapping her in a warm blanket. Gazing down at the little bundle in his arms caused a deep longing within him, an ache for a family of his own. But unless he and Ciara could ever permanently mate, that wish was impossible. And could a mating between a dragon and a lion even produce offspring?

"I found more clothing and a bedding basket we can use for Shuri," Ivran called out as he returned with a basket in his arms.

"Shhhh…she is sleeping," Brenn whispered, looking up at his friend.

"I will set the basket up for her so she can rest," Ivran said in a much softer voice and began removing the clothing and swaddling from the basket. "I also found a couple of toys to hang on the basket, a thicker blanket, and a package of waterproof traveling pants."

Brenn carefully laid Shuri in the basket to nap and turned to his friends. "Come, we have much to discuss before we rest for the night."

They sat at the small table in the kitchen and passed the wineskin around. After each had taken a long drink, Laro looked at Brenn, then Ivran, a ripple running across his features as he fought to keep his lion under control. "My mind is consumed with worry for Tomas. I know he's safe, that Kolin will protect him with his life, but with all that's happened, my lion wants to protect and fight."

"I think this is a problem for all of us, but to change would end this journey. Our families will be lost. I will not let that happen to Reana and Issa." Ivran's whisper ended with his breath catching as he said the names of his mate and child.

Brenn agreed. "We need to travel swiftly. King Biryn needs to know what is happening in the valley, but I am not sure how fast we can climb the ridge with Shuri in tow. She'll need to be fed and changed along the way."

Laro spoke up. "My travels with Tomas were pretty slow at first, but I never ventured over a mountain with him. We will have to fashion a carrier of sorts to strap her to one of our chests. It will keep her comfortable and safe as well as leave our arms free to ride or fight if it comes to that."

Brenn, if you can find a basket with handles, I can safely carry Shuri over the mountain. I can also scout ahead to find a suitable family where you can leave the baby.

Brenn closed his eyes and just drank in the feel of her brushing his mind, then opened them to look at his friends. "Ciara offered to carry Shuri using the bedding basket. This will allow us to reach a farm or the village beyond the ridge before sunset," he told them, heaving a sigh of relief. The baby would have slowed them down far too much.

"Ciara is the dragon? This is the first time I have heard her name." Laro chuckled.

"Please thank her. Shuri will be much safer in flight with the dragon than riding that ridge with us," Ivran said.

"What are your plans once we reach the capital?" Laro asked Brenn as he took another drink of the wine.

"I shall request an audience with King Biryn. He cannot possibly know what has happened yet. The Troncanians could not have vanished more than a few days ago. The baby could not have survived more than that. I am guessing that the disappearance of the Troncanians and our pride happened close in time," Brenn said.

"It has been no more than a week since Xynnar was attacked," Ivran replied as he looked at Brenn. "They were taken two nights prior to you finding me in the forest."

Brenn could not breathe as he realized the night he had spent with Ciara in the Clyss Valley was the night his pride was kidnapped. "I should have been there! I should have kept riding once I escaped the dryons." Instantly, as he uttered the words, he realized if he had tried to continue his journey home, he would not have met Ciara.

"There's nothing you could have done," Ivran said. He offered the wineskin to Brenn. "What did you tell me when I wanted to head out in search of my family? What can we do against the Toubosians and their ships, right? Nothing! We can do nothing. You being there would not have changed anything except you getting captured, too!"

"I agree, Brenn. We could have done nothing against their technology. At least with us free, they have a chance for rescue."

Brenn took a deep breath as he tried to calm his emotions. His lion was so close to the surface that he could feel it clawing for freedom. He shook his head, then drank deeply from the wineskin Ivran had handed him. His mind calming somewhat, he met first Ivran's, then Laro's eyes. "I know you speak the truth. I know we are the best chance they have at freedom."

A lusty wail coming from the bedding basket broke the tension in the room. Laro got up from his chair and went to the cooling box to get a feeding tube and warm it, while Brenn went into the other room to pick up the crying baby.

"I will take care of Shuri while you both get some rest," Brenn said as he walked back into the kitchen with Shuri in his arms. "We must leave early in the morning, and my mind will not allow for sleep."

Laro handed Brenn the warmed feeding tube while Ivran walked into the living area and brought Brenn's bedroll, the bedding basket, and clean swaddling into the kitchen.

"We'll take care of Shuri in shifts. You will need to rest, too," Ivran told Brenn as he handed him a burping cloth.

Brenn agreed as Laro and Ivran made their way into the living area and their bedrolls for sleep.

CHAPTER EIGHT

Brenn watched the sleeping baby in his arms. After a change of swaddling and a feeding tube of jago milk, she had dropped right back into a peaceful slumber. He gazed down at her. So innocent, so unaware of the danger she had been in, and so oblivious to what lay ahead. Softly, he stroked her tiny, balled fist. Shuri stirred, so he withdrew his hand.

He really should lay her down in the bedding basket and get some sleep himself, but holding the sweet little girl helped to calm his shattered emotions. He caressed the leather pouch around his neck. Deep inside he knew he would never be sorry for stopping in Clyss Valley, and that was the crux of the problem.

When had Ciara become more important than his pride, even his own family? After just a week, she had become the center of his world, his soul so tightly bound to hers that if something should ever happen to her, he would be ripped asunder. How could he, trapped as he was, a mere human, possibly keep her safe when he was the one that required *her* aid?

Brenn sighed, stood up carefully with the baby in his arms,

and walked to the bedding basket to lay her down to finish her nap. Then he quietly walked to the large window by the table and looked out at the clear sky. The moons were full and shining brightly as he scanned the fields beyond the barn.

There, under the moons' light, he could see her, the flash of her scales and the silvery purple glow of her reptilian body, standing watch to ensure their safety. Automatically, his hand grasped the leather pouch again, and he whispered her name, Ciara's soul shard so much a part of him now that he sought comfort from her without even realizing what he was doing. He closed his eyes. How could he face his family when he found them, knowing he had not been there to help them when they were taken because he had been enchanted by his siren from the bottomless basin? He could not help but be afraid that he had set everything all in motion by daring to drink from the magical pool.

A soft body pressed against his back, arms snaking around his waist to hold him close. Then a gentle kiss against his shoulder blade.

"Even if you had traveled straight to your village, you could not have saved them," Ciara whispered to him. "If you could even have made it that far. I saw your wounds from the dryons. You were lucky to have made it to Clyss Valley."

Brenn turned in her arms and wrapped her tightly in his embrace. "I cannot help feeling the way I do. I know there is nothing I could have done to change it, and I know that I probably would have perished on the way." He bent his head to bury his face in Ciara's silken tresses. "I do not regret our night together, being with you, but I cannot help wondering if I caused this. No one has ever dared to desecrate the magic of the valley. Could I have done so by making light of it, and therefore my family was taken as punishment?"

Ciara pushed on his chest, then stepped back and looked up, catching his gaze intently. "This started generations before you were born! You did exactly as the gods required you to do. You were *meant* to drink from the Clyss! How could you think for even a moment that the gods would punish you for this! That they would punish innocents. Nothing you could have done would have prevented the destruction of your village or the kidnapping of your people."

Brenn was shocked. "What do you mean by this starting generations ago? Does this have anything to do with you being trapped as a dragon? How could I have been meant to drink from the pool in Clyss Valley?"

"For you to understand, I will have to start with how I came to be considered the beast of the valley, the beast of your legends," she said as tears pooled in her violet eyes. She gazed over his shoulder at the moonlit sky. "Cewrick wants my soul shard, and he will stop at nothing to steal it. I am a sorceress in my own right, but with the spell he placed upon us, I cannot use most of that magick. If Cewrick gains control of my soul shard, he not only gains another black dragon for his army but my powers as well."

She told him about the capture of the jeweled dragons, her family, and friends, about the soul shards and what they meant to the dragons. Then she explained of the spell cast over them that forced them to change and what Cewrick's fierce black dragons really were. "Taylith, my best friend and cousin, sacrificed himself to save me. It is only the goddess' prophecy that kept my mind sane throughout my captivity in Clyss Valley."

Brenn held her in his arms as her body was wracked with sobs, her soul bared to him. Her tearful gaze met his again. "It was you the goddess sent to Clyss Valley to free me. That is why I could shift to this form when you entered the pool. I could not have done so if you were not my lifemate."

Brenn wiped a violet tear from her face. "Is this why we are cursed? If we shift to the lion, why we would not be able to shift back to human?"

Ciara nodded in ascent. "The Crimson Realm was close enough that the shifters there were affected by Cewrick's spell. You would not change into a bastardized version of a lion like the dragons changed into fierce black dragons without any human memory, but you would be trapped as an animal. The valley's magick saved me from such a fate. I kept my human consciousness."

"How is it that you can take your human form? Why are you not bound as a dragon now?"

"When I gave you my soul shard, it allowed me to give you a sliver of my human soul. That is why I can sometimes appear as a human during the night when you call to me. I cannot hold this form for long. When the suns peek over the horizon and begin to rise, I am a dragon once more."

Brenn pulled her to his chest and rested his head on hers. "I am so sorry, my love, for everything that you've gone through, for your imprisonment at the falls, but I will never be sorry that I met you. We will find a way to break this curse, and we *will* find a way to set you and our families free."

A soft sigh and the sound of movement drew their attention to the bedding basket. Ciara quietly walked to the basket and gazed down at the sleeping infant, the little one making sucking noises in her sleep. Ciara smiled and bent down to stroke Shuri's head.

"Do not wake her," he whispered as he came up behind her. He slipped his arms around her waist as she stood back up and leaned into his arms.

"She will rest peacefully for a while until she is hungry. She is beautiful, Brenn."

Her softly spoken words warmed his heart, his soul, erasing some of the sorrow and worry.

"She is, and so innocent and unaware. I hope we find good people to care for her during her parents' absence." Reaching out, he stroked Ciara's hair, trailed his fingers down her cheek, touched her lips. "She causes me to yearn for the impossible, Ciara."

"And that is?"

"You know my mind. A life with you, a family. I do not know what the gods were thinking choosing us to be lifemates. You are bound to your dragon, and even if Cewrick were to be defeated, stripped of his magick, would that erase the curse on you? Enable us to at least be together as a couple?" He sighed. "We could always adopt a child to raise as our own."

Her soft laughter sounded like the tinkling of tiny bells. "Nothing is beyond the power of the gods and goddesses, my warrior. But should it be that we cannot procreate, yes, I would gladly raise an adopted child." She turned in his arms to hug him close. "We are also both human, and as a human, I do not lay eggs. Who knows, we could have a whole litter of lions or a clutch of dragons, or just maybe we will have an interesting mixture of the two." She giggled, then lightly kissed his lips.

"I would not care what they could shift into," Brenn said as he held Ciara close. "My heart is heavy right now with worry over the missing people, and listen to me, concerned about us not being able to have a family. I should be ashamed." She reached up and placed his hand on her chest. He could feel her heartbeat with his fingertips.

"Do not feel shame, my warrior, at opening your heart to me. Come, let us rest. You need sleep before we continue our journey." Ciara led him to the bedroll he had placed on the floor near the bedding basket and urged him to lie down with her.

"I'm just thankful to have found you," he said as he held her in his arms. The steady rhythm of her heartbeat and the warmth of her hand sent him drifting off into a restful sleep.

Shuri's gurgling woke him. Opening his eyes, he sat up and found Ciara gone from his bedroll and the bedding basket empty. He jumped up, following the infant's cooing and Ciara's soft voice, to find them seated in a rocking chair in the corner of the kitchen.

"You slept well, my love. I have swaddled and fed the infant. She, too, slept nearly all night."

"I do not know how she could have survived so many days without sustenance," he said as he gazed down at them both.

"She is strong and resilient but very lucky you found her when you did. I do not think she would have survived another day alone." Ciara continued to rock Shuri as she fed her from a feeding tube, whispering soothingly to her as the baby heartily drank the milk. The sight of her holding Shuri was one he imprinted in his memory. Ciara's face was beautiful, filled with tenderness as she gazed down at Shuri. He wished he was able to sketch, like Obeen, the artist in their village. Obeen could sketch a person's likeness in minutes.

"You are such a sweet girl, little one." Ciara spoke softly to the infant as she continued to rock her gently.

"I will be back shortly," he told her and hurried to relieve himself and wash his face and hands.

When he returned to the kitchen, Shuri lay in the basket, a thumb in her mouth, her eyelids drooping, and Ciara sang softly by her side. Oh, what a sight to behold. As Shuri fell asleep, Ciara stood and dropped the blanket she had wrapped around her body. Naked, she walked to him and into his waiting arms. He held her tightly, wishing the moment to last forever.

"The suns are rising, my love. I must go. My dragon will not fit in this kitchen," Ciara murmured against his chest. "Your friends will wake soon, and you must get ready to eat and travel. Be sure to add extra blankets in the basket. It is much colder up high. Remember to include feeding tubes for her. After I change, I will fly ahead with her, then place the infant with the reliable people I found. I will return to protect you and your friends."

Brenn kissed the top of her head and was about to tilt her face and kiss her on the lips when he noticed the scales getting bigger and a change happening to her body. She stepped out of his embrace and hurried out of the house. As she opened the door, Brenn saw the rising suns and a glimpse of the dragon. He fetched the last of the feeding tubes from the cooler, added swaddling cloths and covered Shuri with another blanket, then took the basket outside.

Ciara flapped her wings and bent her head low. It looked as if the dragon was inspecting the basket. Slowly, she rose up. Brenn set the basket on the ground. Ciara carefully grasped both handles with her forearms, then rose gracefully into the sky. He watched her fly high and away until she was merely a speck against the light of the rising suns.

"You are up early, friend. And you did not wake me for my shift with the infant," Laro said behind him.

"Shuri slept nearly all night. Ciara has already taken her to the other side of the mountains. She has found a family to care for her."

"And pray, how can a dragon do that without being seen?" Laro wondered.

"I do not know. I trust Ciara knows what she is doing. She will return, she told me, and fly with us when we begin today's journey. Is Ivran awake?"

"Yes, and cooking a hearty meal for us. We must be on our way early. The suns are just over the horizon."

They returned to the house. The appetizing aroma of fried meat greeted them. They entered the kitchen to find Ivran had finished cooking breakfast. Brenn's stomach rumbled. "Good morning, Ivran. I trust you slept well?"

Like Laro, Ivran grumbled, "You did not wake me for infant watch. Why?"

Brenn chuckled. "Shuri slept nearly all night. I suppose feeling safe and a full stomach helped to do that." He did not mention that Ciara had been with them throughout the night. "Ciara has already taken Shuri and is flying to the other side of the mountains to place her with a temporary family to take care of her. She'll return to watch over us as we travel."

CHAPTER NINE

After they ate and cleaned up the house, they took some extra food, Brenn making sure to leave some gold coins in the cooler for the family to pay for the provisions they had taken. They saddled their horses, packed the supplies on the packhorse, and rode off the farm to the road leading to the Inar Ridge.

Brenn spotted the dragon flying high above without the bedding basket in her claws. Had Ciara really flown to the other side of the mountains that fast, left Shuri with the temporary family, and returned already?

Oh ye of doubtful mind. Beware as you approach the ridge. I saw some fires and what looked like a spaceship, but I dared not fly close. I left Shuri on the front porch of a stately home. It is located outside of the city limits of Haishing on a large property. Yesterday, when I scouted, I spied on the family—a father, mother, and two younglings. The boy and girl were well cared for. Shuri will be fine with them until we can fetch her and return her to the birth parents.

"Ciara just spoke to me," Brenn told Laro and Ivran.

Laro shook his head in disbelief. "She must truly be magical to be able to speak to you without us hearing her."

"She is. The infant is with an affluent family just outside of

Haishing. Ciara warned of a crashed spaceship on top of the ridge we need to cross."

"It has to be Toubosians. Did she see survivors? If we find a live one, maybe we can get him or her to talk and give us answers," Ivran commented.

"She did not dare fly too close. All she saw was the crashed ship and some fires. Remember, anyone not from our planet could fire upon a dragon, even a beautiful jewel dragon."

"True. At least we are warned, and Ciara will be there to help if needed," Laro said.

They rode hard all day, barely stopping to relieve themselves or rest the horses. Time was of the essence. The longer it took them to reach the capital and speak with the king, the colder the trail to their pride and the Troncanians would be. They arrived at the base of the mountains by mid-afternoon, stopping briefly to eat, drink, and rest the horses before starting the climb.

Brenn finished the chunk of bread and meat, glanced up, and saw Ciara circling high above, ensuring their path was clear of predators. "We need to continue, friends. These mountains are not that steep and the path well-ridden. We should arrive at the ridge before the suns set," he told the men.

They mounted and, with Brenn in the lead, headed up the mountain path. Brenn wondered what lay ahead of them. Were there survivors from the Toubosian ship? Would they be able to interrogate them? His heart pounded at the anticipation of obtaining answers.

When they arrived close to the ridge, it was still daylight. The suns had not yet touched the horizon. Brenn halted Atom. "Whoa, boy. Stop."

"Do you see anything, Brenn?" Laro asked.

"No. I see some areas with smoldering embers, a lot of debris, but no life."

"Should we approach? It does not look like the ship I saw. It is different, and nothing like our own spaceships," Ivran said.

"It could be dangerous to approach on horseback. I am going on foot. You two wait here," Brenn told them.

The crashed ship had sheared a clean path on top of the ridge that led right to it. There was nowhere to hide and approach stealthily. Brenn darted from tree to tree, using the forested side of the mountain as shelter, bush to bush, his gaze was riveted on the ship. There was no movement. Nothing. He had reached the last protective bushes and crouched behind them when suddenly a panel slid open and several figures came into view.

Steps appeared from below the panel to the ground. Fascinated, Brenn watched two men and three women descend. They were human. They could not possibly be Toubosians. Their manner of dress was foreign to him. The women were dressed in some kind of skin that clung tightly to their bodies, the colors bright. The men wore pants that seemed made of the same material, their shirts looser. Their ship was nothing like the ships from the king's space fleet. Who were these people? What planet were they from?

One of them spoke, but Brenn could not understand what they were saying. The language was completely unknown to him.

He was not sure what to do. Should he approach them? He did not want to risk them finding Laro and Ivran if they captured him.

It is safe, Ciara told him.

Okay, so be it. He had to trust Ciara. He left his hiding spot and slowly approached the small group. He saw them instantly reach for what appeared to be some kind of weapon at their sides. Reacting immediately, he reached for his sword.

"Who are you? What are you doing here?" he asked. They

looked at him in confusion, hands still touching the weapons at their sides. Of course — they could not understand him any better than he could understand them.

One of the women spoke, and another woman hastened back toward the ship.

Brenn knew several off-world languages to assist him when participating in negotiation peace conferences for the king, but he still could understand nothing. These people did not seem dangerous. He had seen a lot of different species from other planets, but none that resembled his own pride like these people did. He wondered if they were lion shifters. The woman that entered the ship returned holding a small electronic device. It was very similar to the language translators the king's fleet officers used when visiting other planets. Brenn wished he had thought to keep one in his saddlebag, but he never had a use for one away from the capital. His missions were always on the ground, never in space, though he had been trained for both. And throughout all the realms, the inhabitants spoke Ierilian.

The woman spoke close to the device. Broken up sounds emitted from it. She quickly slapped the device against her leg and spoke close to it again. The garbled sound became a metallic voice that translated her words.

"I am Captain Erica Martinez. This is my first officer, Mark Harris." She indicated the man next to her. "The others are my science officer, Donna Clarke, our doctor, Catrice Parker, and our navigator, Jim Newman. We are from Earth. Where are we?"

"I am General Brenn Mildash of King Biryn the Fifth's mighty legion. These are my friends, Ivran Skullash and Laro Fernwind. This is the planet Ierilia. Where is Earth?"

"Earth is located in the Virgo Supercluster of galaxies. One of our engines malfunctioned, and we were thrown off course. Our ship was hit by a large asteroid and thrown into a wormhole. Our engines were badly damaged, as are our thrusters, and the damage to our ship is irreparable. All communication with Earth and the other ships is lost. We drifted completely off course on the way to the planet Thauro in the Angoro system. We have never heard of Ierilia, but my science officer discovered that your planet's atmosphere is compatible to ours on Earth. We are very lucky to have crashed here, because many planets are not habitable for humans. I feared our last hours had come," the captain replied.

"Are there any casualties?" Brenn asked.

"We have had some casualties, but most of our people are fine. Some have cuts and bruises, but no one is seriously hurt. We lost a large chunk of the storage bays, and a portion of the stasis units were damaged," the captain said into the translation device.

"How many of you are there?" Brenn demanded to know.

"There were thirty-two men and women. We lost four of our crew when some of the stasis units malfunctioned as we were hurled into your atmosphere."

"No children? If you were in stasis, how do you know what happened before waking? What were you seeking on the planet Thauro?" Brenn asked.

"Two of our computer systems are still functioning. One of them recorded everything. There are no children. A few years ago, we discovered Thauro with a space telescope. We then sent probes to the Angoro system and found the planet has a similar atmosphere to Earth and would be habitable for us. We were sent to prepare a settlement for some of the people from Earth to migrate to. Earth is overpopulated, and our ozone layer has been mostly depleted, causing much illness. It has also affected animals and plants. Food had to be rationed. Earth's officials fear the extinction of our race has begun. The only way to ensure our race's survival was to send healthy people to a different planet and establish settlements. Our ship was one of ten sent to Thauro, three of them cargo ships, the others carrying crews to help build the settlement and ready it for Earth's surviving people."

"Do you have enough provisions to stay with your ship? My friends and I do not have enough to feed that many, but we will gladly guide a team down the mountain to our capital, where I am sure the king will offer his assistance. We will be making camp here for the night."

"Thank you for your offer. We have enough provisions for several months, more if we can locate the supplies we lost during the crash."

Brenn turned away from them and motioned Laro and Ivran to join him.

"What do you make of it, Brenn?" Laro asked.

"They are from another planet called Earth. You heard?"

"Some of it. We were too far back. What are they doing here?" Laro asked.

"Their planet is apparently facing the extinction of their race. Their ruler sent this spaceship and the crew, along with a fleet, to another planet to make it ready for Earth's people. Their ship was hit by an asteroid. As you can see, it was mostly destroyed, and they drifted off course and were sucked into our atmosphere."

"They do not look any different from us. Are they lion shifters?" Ivran asked.

"I did not ask that question. Except for the language and their clothing, they look the same as us, but I did not detect the lion scent."

"You are welcome to spend the night on our ship," the metallic voice of the device told them.

Brenn looked at his friends, and both shook their heads. "We are used to sleeping under the moons and stars. Thank you," he responded.

They watched as the people disappeared into the spaceship, then they tethered their horses to a tree and made camp.

"Do you trust them?" Laro asked.

"I do not see why not. Who could make up such a story? Tomorrow, we will talk more with them. I offered to lead them to the capital. The king can decide their fate."

"Fate?" Ivran asked.

"Well, you know what I mean. They said their ship cannot be repaired, so they have no choice but to remain on our planet. We know there are no other planets in our system that could sustain life for us. Since their physiology appears to be similar to ours, taking them to another planet is not an option. I have never heard of their home planet. It must be in another galaxy. We could not assist them to return, should they even want to. They'll need a lot of help from us."

They had just finished building a campfire when the captain approached them. "May my first officer and I join you?" she asked, talking into the device.

Brenn nodded. "Please. Be seated. We would like to learn more about you and Earth." He glanced at the ship and saw the whole crew filing out, looking at them curiously. Several of them sported bandages on their faces or around their heads, and two had an arm bound to their chest in some kind of white cloth.

"Captain, please tell your crew to stay close to the ship. There are predators lurking in the shadows that will kill in an instant," he told her.

The captain nodded and called out to her crew, not using the translator. Brenn noticed the people did not venture far from the ship. He offered the captain food, but she declined.

"Thank you. We have already eaten," she told him.

"Captain—"

"Please, call me Erica."

Brenn smiled. "Erica, we have technology and a space fleet, but we have no idea where Earth is, neither is our technology as advanced as yours appears to be. Our space fleet capabilities do not allow for travel to another galaxy. You and your crew may be permanently stranded on our planet."

Laro and Ivran had been quietly eating and listening until Laro spoke. "Erica, what is this ozone you spoke of?"

Brenn noticed Erica gaze at his handsome friend and saw a spark of interest in her eyes, a spark that seemed to be returned by Laro, the tension between them drawn tighter than a strung bow. *Really? Could this be? Laro finding a mate who has crash-landed from another planet?* He chuckled inwardly. The gods or goddesses were playing games with them. He drank deeply from his wineskin and looked at the group sitting on the ground between them and the ship. They were all busy talking and gesturing, every now and then looking at their captain. He wondered about their conversation.

There are morcougs nearby. They have scented the blood of the deceased that are still on the ship. The bodies must be taken care of right away. Ciara's warning was loud and clear in his mind.

"Erica, there is danger nearby. Warn your crew to return to the ship."

"Really? How do you know? I do not hear or see anything," she responded.

Just after she spoke, Ciara swooped down.

The crew vaulted up and panicked, several of the female crewmembers screaming and running back to the ship. Erica and her first officer drew their weapons and were ready to fire.

Brenn, Laro, and Ivran jumped up and reached for their weapons.

"What are you doing? Stop. I can disintegrate this beast in a second," Erica shouted.

The noise was unbelievable. Men and women yelling,

some screaming, many reaching for their weapons. "Erica, this dragon is friendly. She is here to protect us. Just watch," Laro told her.

Hesitantly, Erica lowered her arm a bit, though not sheathing her weapon. In seconds, Ciara breathed fire into the nearby shrubs and trees, and two roaring morcougs came stumbling out, their fur in flames. Again, Ciara blew fire at them, and they were incinerated within a minute.

Ciara flapped her wings and soared into the sky.

"Now I've seen everything," Erica said and sheathed her weapon. "Dragons on Earth occur only in stories and legends."

"The dragon will watch over us. I advise you to tell your people to bed down for the night, and you and your officer should do the same," Brenn said.

"We have been on the ship for a very long time. Do you mind if we stay with you near your campfire?" Erica asked. "I would like to talk some more."

"I'm bunking down in the ship," Mark said, holding his translator close to his mouth. "Sorry, but that huge dragon freaked me out."

"The dragon is very safe. She watches over us, as you witnessed," Brenn told the man, a little annoyed.

"Nevertheless, I'll bunk down in my cabin. Thank you for your hospitality."

Brenn looked at Erica. "He sounds hostile."

"Please excuse him. His wife was one of the four that did not survive our crash. I would love to hear more about your world. You appear like one of our ancient warriors, as told in legends, yet you speak of spaceships and fleets. I am puzzled," Erica told him.

Laro spoke up. "I'm not a warrior. I am a horse trader."

"And I am a blacksmith. What is wife?" Ivran replied.

"Eh, when a man and a woman join and live together. The

three of you are on a journey to your king. It is an unlikely trio. May I ask why?"

Brenn frowned at Laro and Ivran. He did not want to tell her why they were traveling to see the king. "I was summoned by the king to sit in on a council meeting," he lied. "We made it a hunting journey. Laro and Ivran needed a welcome vacation from their normal duties. Unfortunately, thus far, we have not caught anything."

"But you are enjoying the journey. What about the beasts that just tried to attack? Do you encounter them often?" Erica asked.

"Sometimes. The dragon protects us. Tell us more about this planet you are from," Laro queried.

Conversation was difficult with having to wait for the translator to translate every sentence spoken, but somehow, they managed. Brenn was beginning to feel sleepy, but Erica was wide awake and eager to learn more about them. "We have a long day's ride tomorrow. We should bed down for the night," he warned Ivran and Laro.

Erica looked mortified. "I'm sorry. I am so eager to learn more about you that I'm being rude. I hope you don't mind if I sleep out here with you. Please tell me if you prefer me not to?"

"We do not mind," Laro told her and smiled, indicating a spot not far from him and close to the fire.

One of her crew had brought out what she called a sleeping bag. She spread it out. Again, the interaction between Erica and Laro did not escape Brenn. He had to admit she was a lovely woman, hair the color of the reddish sand near the ocean and green eyes. She wore her hair swept up and tightened to her head. He wondered what she would look like with it hanging loose. Short in stature, slim and very feminine, she nevertheless came across as an imposing figure, and her crew seemed to look up to her.

After adding more wood to the fire, they bedded down for the night. Brenn began to drift off while wondering what the next day would bring.

CHAPTER TEN

Brenn sat up as voices woke him. The suns had barely poked over the horizon. Laro and Erica were quietly talking while several chunks of smoked korobeast warmed over the fire.

"You are up early," Brenn told them as he walked to the fire.

"Well before the suns rose," Ivran grumbled from his bedroll. "Some people like to talk a lot." He glared at Laro.

"Here, try this," Laro said as he handed him a tin cup filled with a hot, dark liquid. "One of her crew brought it out to us. It will wake you up, according to Erica."

Brenn took the cup from him. The scent of the liquid alone made him want to drink from it. It was almost as tempting as the water from the Clyss. He took a tentative sip first, then a large swallow. The experience made him close his eyes in bliss. "What magick is this?"

"No magick." Laro chuckled at his friend. "Erica calls it *coffee*. She says it was made from a plant that grew in abundance on Earth and they have seeds to grow it with them."

"It's a very important crop on Earth. Most would say we couldn't function without it." Erica laughed. "We have plenty of it on board the ship if you would like some for yourselves. It's the least we can do for the help you have offered us."

"Here, taste this," Brenn told Ivran as he handed the cup to him.

Ivran took a sip and sighed in pleasure. "We will gladly take some of this with us."

Erica chuckled at them. "If you like this, just wait until I introduce you to hot chocolate." Brenn and Ivran sat with them by the fire, each taking some of the warmed korobeast. "We must eat quickly and break camp. We have a long day ahead of us if we wish to make it to the base of the ridge," Brenn told them as he watched Laro hand a piece of meat to Erica. Her hair now hung loosely around her shoulders, softening the lines of her face, her eyes sparkling with flirtatious mischief as she took the meat from him. Brenn smiled to himself. *Yes, there is definitely something igniting between those two.*

"Do you have a team ready to travel with us?" Brenn asked Erica as they finished their meal.

"They are waiting by the ship, packed and ready for travel. Laro explained that it would be a day's ride down the mountain. We have packed enough provisions for at least four days. We have no currency, but can trade some of those supplies if needed," Erica informed them as she motioned for her team to join them.

The men broke camp and led their horses to Erica's team. They had met Mark the night before.

"This is Anthony Carmichael, our chief of security," Erica said as she pointed to a tall, muscular man with caramel skin about two shades darker than Shuri's.

"We'll store your supplies on our packhorse. His name is Storm," Brenn said as the team stared at the huge abascos in awe.

"Six legs? That's incredible," Mark said with wonder as he walked up to the horse to help Ivran store their supplies.

"We're going to have to ride double, or we will not make it down the mountain before nightfall. Erica, can you let your crew know to stay on the ship? It would not be safe for them to venture out," Brenn said as he mounted his horse and held his hand out to Anthony to help him mount the horse behind him.

The path is clear. You should not have any trouble going down the path. Ciara's sweet voice brushed his mind.

"Donna, make sure everyone stays on the ship or very close to it. It is not safe to leave the area," Erica said through a small communicator. She seemed to have her translator turned on at all times, so they could understand every word she said.

"You can ride with me," Laro told Erica as he reached out to help her.

Mark climbed on behind Ivran. "I've missed riding," he said wistfully. Then he repeated it into the translator and continued. "My parents owned a farm, but all the horses were taken. All our cattle were confiscated, too. Crops failed. Nothing would grow. The farm became a wasteland, and my parents could not handle the loss. They died within a short time of each other."

Brenn felt really bad for Mark. Not only had he lost his mate, but his parents, too. "I'm sorry," he said into the translator Erica had given him. "When we have more time, I would like to learn how your planet got into this state. I'm sure our king will be very interested to learn this, too."

The path down to the valley was not too steep, but the horses had to carry a double load, so traveling was slower than normal.

The suns were almost touching the horizon when the first town came into sight. Brenn heard Erica gasp. They stopped for a moment to gaze at the city called Haishing. He had to admit it did look fantastic in the rays of the setting suns. She spoke into her translator. "This is magnificent! It resembles a city from the future, science fiction, and you said your technology is limited? We have nothing like this on Earth. Our buildings are primitive compared to this."

"We'll stable the horses first. Then we will continue to my estate in my hovercraft. It is located close to the king's palace. We should arrive in Cront just after the suns have set," Brenn told them.

"We should eat first," Ivran suggested.

"Our rations are almost gone, and I do not care for the Earth rations we tasted at noon. It will not be long before we are in Cront. My staff will prepare a feast for us," Brenn answered.

"Maybe there's an inn nearby?" Laro offered.

"We cannot arrive at an inn with the Earth strangers. My hovercraft is a hundred times as fast as our horses. It will not take long," Brenn promised.

Erica spoke into her translator. "There's always coffee. It fixes everything. It will even still hunger temporarily." She took a long, oval container from her pack, unscrewed the top that looked like a short cup, then poured steaming liquid into it and handed it to Laro.

"An interesting concept," Laro said as he drank the coffee. "I could get very used to this liquid."

Mark and Anthony produced their flasks and handed coffee around. After they all had two cups, Brenn led them to the stables and paid the stable hand to take care of the horses. "Tharno, please have the horses transported to my estate after they have been fed and rested."

Brenn motioned to the others. "Follow me. My craft is parked in the hovercraft holding chamber." He opened a door and waited for them to come in. Again, gasps from the Earth people.

"This can't be real," Erica exclaimed, running a hand over Brenn's bright yellow, shiny craft. "It has no wheels. Why do you ride horses if you have a hovercraft to use? Travel would be much faster and less dangerous."

Brenn laughed. "We have seen no wheels on crafts in the city for many centuries. Only farmers use carts with wheels, but that's all on the other side of the mountains." He chose not to divulge the reaction of technological devices to the koriam crystals, so he lied. "As for the horses, we prefer to ride them when we visit home. It is a nice change from the bustle of the city."

He constantly had to remember to hold the translator close to his mouth. Waiting for the translation was a nuisance. He hoped these people were smart enough to pick up on their language fast. "Please, get in. I'm anxious to go home to a hot bath and a hotter meal."

He uttered a command, and four doors opened from bottom to top. As usual, the craft asked for his destination. "Home to Cront," he commanded. Using the craft's datapad, he sent a message to the king. Then he relaxed in his seat for the ride home.

"I think we died, and this is Heaven," Erica said as she stood on the porch of Brenn's mansion, looking at his vast estate. "It has to be a hallucination. A dream. None of this can be real. We crashed, and we're all dead. Look at those gardens, the sea of flowers, those trees. Oh, wow, look at the trees way in the back. They're laden with fruit unlike we've ever seen. It's breathtaking."

Brenn's home was built on a hill. It was a mixture of technological advancement and old world. The exterior looked lavish, built with blue-and-gray granite. Large round windows added to its charm. He owned a good portion of land with stables, gardens and orchards, and housing on it for his staff. The estate had been gifted to him by the king as a reward. Brenn was the first in his family to own such splendor.

"Far from dead. If you would like to follow me into the house, you can bathe and refresh before we dine. Your quarters are ready. I instructed my staff before we arrived."

"How?" Erica asked.

"So many questions. All in good time. For now, we will bathe, dine, and relax. Tomorrow morning, we have an audience with the king. I've already issued my request."

Erica cast him a sidelong glance. "And how do you know the king will honor your request?"

"I am his general. The king knows if I request an audience, it is of importance. Now go. My staff is waiting to assist you."

After each had followed a staff member to their designated quarters, Brenn headed for his own. He could hardly wait to relax in the perfumed waters of his baths, to have a pretty servant massage his muscles, oil his body, wash his hair. At times they had pleasured him, but now he was bound to Ciara. He had no desire for anyone but her.

He dared not linger in the baths for too long. After he had stepped out, a jet stream of air dried his long, tousled hair. Chath, a pretty blonde who was the usual female who looked after his needs, carefully combed it until it hung in waves over his shoulders. His clothes were ready. For that evening, he did not bother with his official attire. He put on dark blue pants, then a light blue tunic edged with gold braid. Slipping into sandals, he quickly left the room and headed for the dining room to find everyone there waiting for him.

"What took you so long? I am starved," Laro grumbled.

"Sorry. The bath felt so good, I could have stayed in it much longer." Brenn noticed Laro and Ivran had made use of the clothing left for them, but the Earth crew still wore their uniforms.

Using the translator, he said, "I hope you feel refreshed? Our meal will be served now."

He had no sooner spoken when servants filed in carrying large platters laden with food. They placed them on the table and stood back.

"Can we ask what we are eating?" Erica asked.

Brenn picked up his translator. "You can, but the words or names will be foreign to you. Much of it is meats and vegetables. There's some fish, too. You can have a small taste. We'll not be offended if you do not like it, but after us trying your rations, I think you will be pleasantly surprised."

Brenn was glad when everyone had had their fill and mentioned they were tired. He wanted nothing more than to retire to his chambers. He had not been home for a long time, and between the war and his travels back to his birth home, he looked forward to relaxing in his own bed for the night.

He undressed and was about to relax naked on his bed when he noticed a glow on the fields of his estate. Jumping up, he ran to the verandah and saw her in all her magnificence. But in seconds the dragon disappeared. In its stead, a woman ran toward his home. A siren, in all her naked glory, her long raven hair flying behind her, her silvery skin aglow. Ciara. His lifemate. His love. The sight held him in thrall just as it had when he first saw her in the Clyss. She drifted up to the verandah and landed to stand before him. He reached out, and she walked into his embrace.

"We have this night, my love," she whispered against his neck.

Brenn held her close just breathing in the scent of her skin. "I have so longed for you, Ciara, but so many other matters interfered." He bent down and sought her lips with his, placing a tender kiss on them, then looked up and caught her gaze. "The worrying about my family and members of my pride, the disappearance of the people from the other village, and now these people from another planet… My brain is too busy with it all."

Ciara caressed his cheek, caressing him with her fingers from his strong jaw to the base of his neck and back. "Brenn, you are the answer. You released me from the Clyss. You will find the missing people. Do not worry about the foreigners. They will settle on Ierilia and even become helpful in many matters. Let me erase your worries for this night. Allow me to pleasure you as you should be by your mate." She slid her hand down his chest and lower until she was cupping him gently in her hand.

Brenn moaned at the feel of her hand on him, her touch setting his skin ablaze, his cock beginning to throb with need. Kissing her hungrily on the lips, he disengaged her hand from his cock, scooped her up into his arms, and carried her to his bed. His cock felt like it would burst, but he would pleasure her first. His lips sought hers again, kissing her tenderly. Then he kissed her nose, her ears, and trailed kisses down her neck, nipping and licking her silvery scales all the way to her pert nipples.

Taking his time, he teased and kissed the scales around her areolas. He sucked first one, then the other nipple into his mouth, biting the little points, then soothing them with his tongue. Her body arched below him, her hips seeking his cock, her hands urging him on.

He continued his exploration of her scales, first softly scraping with his teeth, then licking her skin down to her bellybutton, stopping long enough to kiss it, then continued down to the soft hair of her mound.

Slowly parting her legs, he kissed a trail along the inside of her thigh all the way to her clitoris. It was hard and throbbing and begging for his touch. He played with it using his tongue, circled it, then sucked it hard into his mouth. He heard her gasp in pleasure at the sensual onslaught, as her hips arched to meet his teasing tongue.

"Please, Brenn...I need you."

He entered first one finger, then two, pumping them in and out and slowly swirling them around inside her wet opening. He continued to tantalize her clitoris with his tongue as she writhed against him. He sat on his knees between her spread legs and gazed down at his beautiful siren. Her long hair was splayed across the pillows, those delicate scales shimmering in the moonlight. She bit her lip enticingly as her body bucked in time to the thrust of his fingers. Gods, she was a beautiful sight. He watched as he moved his fingers in and out of her tight sheath, her nectar flowing freely down his hand.

She was ready. Oh, so ready. Slowly, he removed his fingers, lifted her ankles over his shoulders, and looked at her face. She opened her eyes as he positioned his cock at her entrance. Her eyes were the deepest purple, her luscious lips slightly parted, her hips bucking to meet him.

He inched in, slowly, bit by bit, torturing her. He heard her moan in pleasure, in agony as she tried to force him fully into her, but still he taunted her relentlessly.

Suddenly, she withdrew from him and crept back toward the head of the bed. Her head swung wildly around.

"Ciara, what is wrong? What did I do?"

She grasped her head with her hands as if in pain. "My love, it is not you. The crew on the spaceship. They did not listen to their captain. They ventured outside into the forest and are in grave danger. I have to go and help them."

His ardor fully doused, Brenn sank back onto the bed and watched helplessly as his siren jumped off the bed and ran to the verandah. In a second she leaped over the balustrade and was gone.

He followed and stood on the verandah, watching the dragon as she flew away. "What just happened?" he muttered. She had gone to help the crew from the spaceship.

Why were they outside? Why had they disobeyed their captain? He thought about seeking out Erica to have her talk to her crew. But how could he explain how he knew? He had to leave it in Ciara's hands. Troubled, he returned to his bed, pulled up the covers, and tried to sleep. When he finally drifted off, he was restless, and he constantly woke up, expecting to find Ciara back in his arms.

CHAPTER ELEVEN

B renn was awake before the suns rose. What had happened the night before plagued his mind. Were the people from Earth okay? Had Ciara saved them? Why were they so stupid to leave the spacecraft when they were told not to? The questions roiled in his mind. He walked to the window overlooking the field Ciara had appeared in the night before. There was no sign of her.

He bathed, then dressed in his official uniform — tight black pants and a long-sleeved, velvety blue jacket buttoned to just below his waist. The jacket had a rectangular neckline and gold braiding on the shoulders. Beneath, he wore a stylish white shirt. He clasped the dark leather belt with a gold buckle around his waist. It always made him feel like he was in a harness. It had a gold insignia on it, indicating his status and wealth. Last, he put on the hard leather boots. He really hated the constriction of the uniform and was always glad to take it off again. Thankfully, he did not have to wear it to battle. When he went downstairs to the dining room, he was surprised to find Ivran and Laro already there. The Earth crew was still asleep, he guessed.

He greeted his friends. "Good morning. We have a development. Apparently, Erica's crew disobeyed her and decided to venture out of the ship late last night. Ciara sensed danger and had to go to their rescue. I've had no word on how this turned out."

Laro frowned. "And you know this how?"

"Ciara told me. Somehow she knew they were in trouble."

"What was the danger?"

"I have no idea. Until I hear from Ciara, I cannot tell you anything."

Erica joined them. She held the translator close and said, "Good morning. I had disturbing news from one of my crew members. They were attacked last night by some monstrous creatures."

"Was your crew warned not to venture out of the ship?" Brenn said.

"Yes. And I'm more than angry. No one was killed, thank goodness. There were some injuries. The doctor is dealing with those. Apparently, your dragon came to the rescue. I would really like to know more about this dragon and why it's watching my people."

Brenn shrugged. "You should be glad it *is* watching your people."

"Sounds like morcougs," Laro said.

"Could be. We will not know until we hear from Ciara."

He had not used the translator when he said that because he did not want Erica to know that he had a personal relationship with the dragon.

"What did you say?" Erica asked.

"Sorry. It could have been morcougs. The same creatures that were stalking your people when we arrived. That's what I said."

At the same time, he wondered how Ciara had known that those people were in danger. Then again, she had told him she was a sorceress. When the morcoug had split open his chest, she had sensed the danger he had been in, but he knew she could not have the same connection to the Earth people that she had with him. There were many mysteries his love had yet to reveal.

My love, the Earth people need to move the bodies of the dead into the open so that I can burn them to ash. The scent is attracting quartz lions and morcougs. I see them prowling. If I do not do something about it now, I fear they will be attacked by one or both.

Brenn closed his eyes and took a deep breath, so relieved to feel her presence in his mind.

"Where are you keeping the bodies of your dead?" he asked through the translator.

"They're in the cold storage room until we can bury them properly," Erica replied, the translator close to her mouth.

"You must tell your crew to bring the deceased out into the open. The bodies must be incinerated. They cannot be buried. You risk morcougs ripping through the hull to get at them and your crew, as well as other predators that are attracted by the scent prowling the area."

"But they are behind steel doors. How can they smell the bodies and how will we incinerate them?"

Ivran brought up his own translator. "Your ship is no longer airtight. Between the heat of our atmosphere and your crash landing, the metal and construction of your ship were weakened, and the integrity of your airlocks was compromised. Morcougs are creatures with immense strength. They can break through almost anything."

Erica looked at him in surprise. "How could you possibly know about the metal and construction of our ship?"

"I work metals. Because I choose to forge it in the old way does not mean I am not trained in our modern technologies," Ivran said, shrugging.

"Contact your people. Have them bring the bodies away from the ship to the clearing where we camped yesterday. The dragon will incinerate them for you," Brenn told her.

"How can you know the dragon will do that?"

"Just do it before you lose more of your crew."

Erica looked at him steadily, frowning slightly, then spoke into her communicator. "Donna, get a security crew together and remove our deceased to the clearing where the Ierilians camped last night."

"Captain? What about a service for them?" a woman said through the communicator.

"No questions, Donna. Just do it! Quickly!"

"Aye, Captain."

After a few moments, Donna's voice came back through the communicator. "A security detail is relocating the bodies now, but why are we moving them? We cannot bury them yet, and I'm afraid more of those huge creatures will return. We can't just leave them out there to be eaten by them."

"Brenn told me the dragon will incinerate the bodies. The scent is attracting predators. I fear something worse may find the ship and attack. I refuse to lose any more of you."

"No! There will be nothing left of her!" Mark exclaimed as he ran into the room, Anthony following close behind. "You can't do this!"

"Mark, think rationally," Anthony told him as he walked to stand beside him. "We don't know what type of creatures make this planet home. For God's sake, there's a dragon following us. What the fuck would happen to our people if something much worse attacked? With the damage the ship sustained in the crash, the walls won't keep a large predator out. They'll be sitting ducks!"

Brenn had understood most of their words through the translator and turned to look at them both. He could not bear the thought of losing Ciara, so he understood Mark's pain. Mark's wounds were raw. He would want to memorialize his fallen wife. Brenn spoke into the translator. "Mark, this is not something we wish to do, but it must be done. Was your wife wearing anything that you would like to keep? Once the dragon breathes fire upon the bodies, there will be nothing left."

Mark closed his eyes, his face contorting in pain. "Amanda wears a locket around her neck," Mark said into the translator. "It contains a picture of her and an image of our unborn baby. I would like it back." He looked at Erica, unshed tears pooling in his eyes. "Please, Erica, have them remove it and place it in my cabin and ask them to collect her ashes and put them into a container?"

Brenn saw Erica's breath catch in her throat as her gaze locked with Mark's. "Donna, go and remove Amanda's locket from around her neck before the dragon incinerates the bodies! And collect the ashes of all four crew members into separate containers so we can give them a proper burial. Use the metal containers from sick-bay," she ordered into the communicator. She turned back to Mark. "Amanda was pregnant? Why didn't you say something?"

"What good would it have done? Catrice knew," Mark whispered, his anguish causing his voice to break up.

"I retrieved Amanda's necklace and placed it on the bureau in Mark's cabin," Donna said. "The dragon is burning the bodies now."

"Thank you, Donna, and for God's sake, please keep everyone inside the ship after this is done! This is not a request. It's an order," Erica commanded.

"Aye, Captain!" Donna responded.

Brenn was glad that most of the time the Earth crew kept the translators close, so he caught most of what was said. Erica's face had remained firm, almost cold, during the interaction with Mark and her crew, but Brenn read the anguish in her eyes. She was not as tough and stern as she portrayed. He fully understood. He led a large army and had to maintain a tough image for his warriors at all times, even if his heart shattered at the death of one or more of his fighters.

Such was the role of a good leader.

"King Biryn does not like to be kept waiting. Food is waiting to be served, and then we must be on our way. Please sit," he told them all.

CHAPTER TWELVE

T he guards flanking the huge palace doors swiftly jumped to attention as Brenn approached, followed by the others. "At ease." Brenn touched his left shoulder in greeting as was the custom.

Erica spoke softly into her translator. "I've never seen such splendor. On Earth, we have palaces that were built centuries ago. This futuristic version of a palace is beyond anyone's imagination."

Brenn had to admit she spoke the truth. Biryn's palace was one of serene beauty. Built completely from marble and what looked like a crystal material, its exterior glimmered and sparkled in the light of the suns.

The guards opened the doors to allow them entry. Brenn marched ahead—he knew the way to the throne room all too well. When in private counsel, the king always had Brenn come to his private quarters, treating him more as a friend than his general. But this situation was different, so Brenn had requested an official meeting. The king's advisor and his council would be in attendance when Brenn presented Erica, Mark, and Anthony.

The interior was decorated with elegant space-age furniture. Octagon windows sent plenty of sunlight into the great hall, lighting up the gemstones embedded beneath the clear surface of the floor. Images of former kings, queens, princes, and princesses were displayed as holograms on both sides of the hall.

The king's guards opened the gilded doors to the throne room as the small group approached. Their curious glances at the Earth people did not escape Brenn.

King Biryn did not wait for Brenn to approach and greet him in a formal manner. He was a young king, close to Brenn's age. He jumped up and ran down the steps toward his general. "I'm so glad to see you, my friend. I've missed you."

Brenn chuckled as he stepped out of the king's arms.

"I had expected you after your return from battle. I know, I know. Do not even say it. I gave you permission to visit your family first. But what have we here?" King Biryn looked beyond Brenn's shoulder.

"One of the reasons for an official meeting, Your Majesty," Brenn said. He handed the king a translator. King Biryn looked at it curiously.

"This button is to listen, and this one to speak into the translator." Brenn showed the king.

The king swung around and headed back to his throne. "General, please explain."

Brenn told of the crashed spaceship, then introduced the three people from Earth to the king.

"I would like the captain to tell her story. Captain Martinez, please speak."

Erica startled out of her awe at the splendor of the throne room and began to step forward, but Brenn gently stopped her. She bowed, then began to tell the king everything, from their equipment malfunctioning, being hit by the asteroid, hurled into the wormhole, and what all happened after that.

The king was quiet for a few moments, then spoke. "You

and your crew have been through quite an ordeal. You do realize we are unable to help you return to your universe? We have never heard of your planet or your galaxy. There are countless wormholes, but entering them is very dangerous, as you experienced, and you could be thrown anywhere, even into a black void. Our technology is far advanced, but there is no machinery able to pinpoint other galaxies. Not yet."

"Your Majesty, I do realize our predicament. Your planet is compatible, and with your permission, we are willing to make our home here. We have brought along many seeds, plants, and technology from Earth that did survive the crash. Unless you know of another hospitable planet with the same atmosphere and you could relocate us?" Erica said.

"Captain, there are no other planets in this galaxy that can sustain human life. We have visited some, but we have to wear suitable protective clothing and oxygen tanks, as do alien visitors when visiting Ierilia. You and your crew are welcome to make your home on Ierilia. We will assist you, teach you our language, our customs, and I will assign you living quarters."

"Thank you, Your Majesty. If possible, we would like to remain together."

"For now, you will live in a learning compound within the city. I will place Councilman Trevarto in charge of your group and the arrangements. After you have settled, learned our ways and language, you can advise us what you would like."

"After we've learned the language and culture, would it be possible for my crew and I to find work?"

"Captain Martinez, there are always openings in my space fleet. Or, if you so desire, you can work anywhere in our city, or you can settle on farms. You have much to think about and decisions to make. I would request you to change your attire. You will draw too much attention wearing your Earth clothing."

He stopped and looked at Brenn. "General, speak to my fleet admiral and have him ready two hovercrafts to transport the captain's crew from the ridge. Also, two cargo shuttles for their belongings and the cargo the captain spoke of, though I want our biologists to study your cargo for possible contamination. A single cell microscopic organism-like bacteria could contaminate our own crops or bring disease to our planet. With your permission, Captain? If you do not allow this, we will have to destroy your cargo."

Erica nodded. "Yes, Your Majesty. Of course. On Earth, we would do the same."

"You and your crew will first be transported to our medical facility to be examined. Do you agree?"

"Yes, Your Majesty."

The king nodded to one of his council members. "Trevarto, you know what to do." He looked at Erica. "Please accompany Councilman Trevarto."

"We will meet again," Brenn said and handed his translator back to Erica. Laro and Ivran did the same.

The king had joined Brenn and stood beside him, watching the group leave the throne room. "Your Majesty, I have other matters to speak to you about. But can we do this in private for now? I will need Ivran and Laro to accompany us."

"Of course. Come with me," the king said, placing an arm around Brenn's shoulders.

Once in the king's private quarters, he motioned them to sit, then filled four goblets with wine. He handed a goblet to each of the men and held his up. "A toast to victory and resolved matters." They toasted back and sipped from the wine. "And now, what is it you wish to speak to me about, Brenn?"

"Your Majesty—"

"Brenn, we are in my private quarters. No need to be formal, my friend," the king interrupted.

"Biryn, I bring sad and troubling news." He told the king everything that had happened, including the dragon, but left personal details out.

"A jewel dragon? So they are not a legend after all. I have had peaceful negotiations with the Toubosians, although I have never completely trusted them. I have always found very little humanity in their nature. They are more reptilian and cunning. Why would they abduct all the people from two villages and burn one to the ground? It does not make much sense," the king said.

"We have come up with some possibilities. One is that their leader is in league with Cewrick," Brenn said.

The king's face went red at the name. "Cewrick! That sorcerer will be the death of me yet. He has not caused any problems for a very long time. Why now? And what could he and the Toubosians possibly want?"

"The Toubosians could covet the ore from Xynnar and Troncania. Perhaps they want to build the ultimate weapon or use it for their existing weapons," Ivran suggested.

"It still does not make sense. Why would Cewrick be interested in this? All that murderer has to do is use his black dragons and his magick. Why abduct the villagers? Burn one village to the ground? There has to be more to this." The king ran his fingers through his long brown hair.

"We suspect the Toubosians are hiding in the Sucronian Mountains. I need to rescue my family and our friends. But we need your space warriors and fleet for that," Brenn said.

The king stood and began pacing. "You realize if we attack, they could kill the captives, if they're even on their spaceships. They could have been taken to Cewrick's castle. An attack could also instigate a full-scale war—a war we would win, I am sure, but at the cost of many lives. We need to handle this very carefully."

"A thought just occurred to me. Barely anyone knows

about the secret experiments with the ore from Xynnar and Troncania. Ivran and Laro had no idea. I have never told anyone, as you told me in complete confidence what our scientists were experimenting with. But there were some that did know, a few mining officials in Xynnar and Troncania. Could we have a traitor in our midst?" Brenn offered.

"That still does not explain the abduction of the people or the destruction of your village," the king answered.

"True. It could become a hostage situation — the formula in exchange for our people," Laro said.

The king shook his head. "We are only speculating that Cewrick has a hand in this. I honestly cannot see how any of it would interest him. You were wise to bring this up in private, Brenn. A traitor is not so farfetched. There could even be one among my council. And that brings me to another thought. Cewrick could be involved wanting to overthrow me and gain control over our planet."

"First, we need to find out where they are holding our people," Brenn said.

"Brenn, you are to gather your most trusted officers, take one of our stealth ships that you can cloak, and go and search for the Toubosian ships. You were trained for our space program, too, so here is your chance to prove yourself in a different area of warfare," the king said.

"I want to help. My mate and infant were taken. I served my time in your army and received space training," Ivran offered.

Laro stepped up. "As did we all. I am in. My parents, family, and friends are all missing. I have as much interest in this as Brenn."

"So it shall be. Not a word of this to anyone. I do not know who we can trust at this point."

Brenn sighed. "Biryn, I cannot just walk in and grab a spaceship. Some of your space officers will need to receive orders from you. You will need to come up with a reasonable explanation. And I would rather take my two friends here along. I can trust them with my life."

The king stopped pacing and grabbed Brenn's shoulders. "You should be my advisor. Not that old man I have now. The commanding officer of the fleet will be told that I'm sending you on a peace mission to negotiate trade terms with the ruler of Texnania."

"We've never had dealings with that planet," Brenn said.

"Exactly. But of late, there has been some contact. So your mission would not seem strange. When you leave here, you will go directly to Admiral Zhala. He is the only one I can trust, and he will have received his orders before you arrive. I will inform him of everything. Now, before you depart, tell me more about the Clyss and your magical dragon. I'm mystified by it all."

Brenn told as much as he could, leaving out that Ciara could take human form and mated with him, that she was his lifemate. That could come later. "I do not think she will appear above the city unless she has to. It could cause a panic," he concluded.

"And you are able to communicate with the dragon?" Biryn asked.

"She speaks in my mind. Before Cewrick's curse, she was capable of much magick."

Ivran interrupted. "I witnessed some of it. Her tears healed Brenn. He should have died of his wounds. Now, he has no mark on his chest where it was splayed wide open."

"Remarkable. The legends of the jewel dragons are all true, then. Maybe your dragon can tell us why Cewrick turned on her species so many centuries ago. The legends tell us the dragons inhabited the Tideless Abyss, rich in gemstones of great value and priceless metals. As you know, no one can venture there. I want to know more, but now, it is time for you three to leave. Go directly to Admiral Zhala and begin your mission. May the gods and goddesses protect you. I will do my work here on the ground to find a possible traitor."

On their way out of the castle and to Brenn's hovercraft, Laro suddenly said, "Maybe when we were in the king's army we were trained for both ground and space warfare, but we need a pilot."

Brenn laughed as he opened the doors of his craft. "I was trained in all aspects of space warfare. That includes piloting a ship."

Laro grunted. "But you are probably completely out of practice."

CHAPTER THIRTEEN

"**S**ee, Laro, I have not forgotten my training," Brenn said and laughed. "Do you really think the king would have sent me on this mission if I could not handle it?" He was glad they had stopped on his estate long enough for him to change out of his constricting uniform. They were the same height and build, so he provided Ivran and Laro with suitable clothing. The black battle suits the three of them were wearing suited the type of mission they were preparing for.

"Sorry."

Brenn was surprised that Admiral Zhala himself waited for him near the stealth ship. "Greetings, Admiral. It has been a long time."

"Brenn, yes, it has. The king has filled me in with a few details, and I have decided to accompany you. It has been far too long since I have been on a mission, and the king told me this one is of the utmost importance. I have missed my space missions. Sitting in an office giving orders is not much to my liking."

Brenn introduced Laro and Ivran.

"Admiral, are you comfortable with this boy piloting this ship?" Laro asked while taking his seat in the ship, causing the admiral to burst into laughter.

"It is okay. I know you are uncomfortable flying above ground. Admit it." Brenn glanced at Laro, who sat behind him.

Admiral Zhala had given Brenn curious glances. He was obviously puzzled. But he was a trusted officer in charge of the king's fleet and protection teams and would never question the king. He had started his service when the king's father was still alive.

Brenn looked at the controls. Nothing much had changed since his training, and the ship would almost fly itself after he set the coordinates.

I will be flying beside you, my love.

With everything that had gone on that morning, Brenn had not had time to think much about Ciara except for when he was talking to the king about the jewel dragon. Somehow, she knew what had transpired between them and the king and knew of his mission. For a moment, he thought about the people from Earth, but he knew they were in good hands. There was no need to worry about them.

They lifted off. "Looking a little green there, Laro," Brenn joked.

"I am fine," Laro responded and grunted.

Ivran chuckled.

"I will get back at you two. How long until we get there?" Laro asked.

"In this? Faster than you can imagine. I'm cloaking the ship now so no one can see us."

I can see you. I cannot cross into the Sucronian Mountains with you, but I will wait for you at the border. If I fly close to Cewrick's castle, it will give him control over me. You hold my soul shard now, so he can never get that unless he captures you. But he could stop me from leaving the mountains and bind me to remain there.

Ciara, do not endanger yourself. I shall be fine.

I love you, my warrior prince.

"I am not a prince." Without thinking, he had said it aloud.

"What?" Laro uttered.

Ivran said, "Huh?"

You are my prince.

Brenn concentrated on his flight path. The knowledge that she was flying beside him felt good, but he worried about her. She should not be putting herself in such danger flying so close to Cewrick's domain on his account. If she was captured, there was nothing he could do to save her aside from a full-scale attack on Cewrick. He could not help but feel that their relationship was very much one-sided when it came to the strength to protect. *I should be guarding her.* His pride wounded, he hated the feeling of helplessness that was plaguing him. From the moment he had seen the remains of his village, he had felt as if he were a pawn in a dangerous game of chess.

"Brenn, what are you thinking about? What's this about a prince?" Ivran asked.

"Oh, never mind. We are almost above the castle. I see a lot of black dragons."

Laro peered at the view screen. "Can they see us?"

"No. We are cloaked, invisible. If the Toubosians are hiding here, they would be in the mountains behind the castle. We are almost above them," Brenn said.

Ivran suddenly shouted, "Look, I see them. Three ships. Just like I saw when it happened. One ship close to the ground, and two hovering above."

Brenn looked at the screens. "I see no activity, no sign of any life forms. The scanner is not picking up any signs of life within the ships."

"What does that mean?" Laro asked.

"That our people are not on those ships, but neither are there any Toubosians," Brenn said.

"So where are they?" Ivran asked.

"Somewhere in Cewrick's castle," Brenn answered grimly.

"Unless he killed them all or turned them into something else," Laro said somberly.

"Let us not think the worst, Laro. Cewrick usually has an agenda. He might have turned the Toubosians into soldiers to work for him." Brenn did not know if his attempt to soothe worked. Ivran's next comment let him know it had not.

"But what about our people? My mate, my baby?"

"We do not even know if Cewrick has our people. We are grasping at a thin straw and making wild guesses. We need to investigate further. That is the purpose of our mission," Brenn said in a firm tone.

"And how do we go about doing that?" Laro asked.

"We need to get into Cewrick's castle."

"Oh, just like that. If it were all that easy, why did the king not defeat and annihilate the evil sorcerer before now?" Laro grumbled.

Admiral Zhala leaned over to speak to Laro. "Cewrick has many followers that worship him and would like to see him overthrow the king. He has sent some of his minions to all corners of our planet to drip poison in our people's ears. He has also made promises beyond belief. We have caught several of the upstarts, and they broke under interrogation. It was wise of King Biryn not to annihilate him prematurely, although I doubt he could. It is no mean task to overthrow a sorcerer as powerful as Cewrick. This region would become extremely unstable. We have no wish to start a large-scale civil war."

Brenn looked at the admiral. "I agree, but that does not stop our present need to infiltrate Cewrick's castle."

Admiral Zhala smiled at Brenn. "This is where I may be of assistance. I have several spies within Cewrick's walls. I have not wanted to risk their safety by making contact too soon, but I am scheduled to meet with one of them this evening at the Gilded Arrow Inn on the outskirts of Branton. It is possible she may have information regarding your people."

"I'm curious how you managed to infiltrate Cewrick's castle since we cannot enter the Forbidden Forest."

"Elasha pretended to become Cewrick's follower. His minions are able to navigate the forest safely. He probably has a protection spell around them or something. After we meet with her, I'm not sending her back in."

"We'll attend this meeting with you."

Admiral Zhala looked as if he would argue, but Brenn silenced him. "I will have it no other way. Our people's lives depend on this information. We will ensure the safety of your spy."

The admiral bowed his head in acquiescence, "I agree with your terms. But before we meet with her, we need to make absolutely sure she was not followed."

"Agreed," Brenn said as he turned back to the ship's console and flipped several switches on the panel. "Admiral Zhala, please take the flight controls. I need to inform the king of our plans. I will return shortly."

The admiral took over piloting as Brenn moved to a private room within the ship, seated himself before the communications console, and sent a quick missive to the king for a private conversation. Within moments, King Biryn's face appeared on the screen.

"What news do you have of your surveillance mission?"

"We have located three Toubosian ships hidden behind the castle in Cewrick's courtyard. There is no movement around them, and our scans did not pick up life forms within the ships. We can only assume that the Toubosians and our missing people are within Cewrick's castle. We will be meeting with a spy Admiral Zhala planted within Cewrick's household. It is our hope that she will have information of where our people may be hidden."

"I had hoped your suspicions of the Toubosians was wrong. Our trade agreements have been beneficial to both planets. Forward the surveillance images to me. I want proof of their ships' location when I contact Empress Khatari. She has to know this act of aggression against us will not go unanswered!"

"Do not do anything rash, Biryn. We do not want to give away too many secrets when you speak to the Toubosian ruler. I would withhold information of the attack on my home and the kidnapping of our people. Let her assume you have not received news of this yet. We have yet to hear what the admiral's spy has to say."

"Again, you are wise to council me. I will explain the footage as a routine surveillance mission. I had suspicions that Admiral Zhala had a spy network within Cewrick's realm. He's very resourceful and more than overprotective of my well-being."

"I have only met him in passing, but I agree with his handling of your safety. From what I've heard, he was almost killed when General Thulla assassinated your father and then tried to kill you."

"Yes, he was. He took the shots that were meant for me. If not for him, the plot to overthrow my family would have come to fruition. I trust him implicitly. That is why I requested that he, himself, handled your mission. Transmit the live images to me. Contact me again after you speak with Zhala's spy."

Brenn watched the screen as King Biryn's face disappeared from the viewer. Then he located the surveillance feed of the Toubosian ships and sent it directly to the king. Biryn's reassurance of his trust in Admiral Zhala helped to settle his unease about the man being so closely involved in the investigation. There were rumors of shifters, legends passed down through the generations, but no actual proof they existed. It was a secret they kept close to their hearts. King Biryn, of course, knew of their existence as well as a very select few high-ranking officials, but he feared what news they might receive could expose them as shifters to Admiral Zhala.

Brenn absently touched the pouch around his neck, thinking of his beautiful Ciara. Worry pierced him at her proximity to Cewrick's realm. His pride pricked at the idea that she was the one that constantly had to come to his rescue, that she knew when he was in danger, but he had no sense of when she could be in trouble. He had heard nothing from her since they had flown above the Forbidden Forest and neared Cewrick's castle.

I am safe, my love. I am well hidden and await your return. I will not put myself in unnecessary danger.

Brenn sighed in relief as her reassuring words filled his mind.

"Thank you," he whispered as he left the private room to join the others at the front of the ship.

When he took his place at the console, Brenn noticed Admiral Zhala had already punched in the coordinates for Branton and the Gilded Arrow. It only took minutes in the spaceship. They landed, still cloaked, on a bare strip of land close to the inn.

Brenn turned to his friends. "You wait here for us — we should not be too long."

He followed the admiral, and as they approached the back of the inn, he heard him speak. "Elasha. Are you there? We are outside the inn, at the back. I do not think it is safe to meet inside, in case some of Cewrick's minions are there. I'm sure you do not know them all."

Brenn glanced around but saw no movement anywhere. If the spy had been followed at all, they had probably followed her inside. Unless Cewrick was suspicious of her, Brenn even doubted that she had been followed. But one never knew. "All is clear out here. How are you communicating with Elasha?" he asked the admiral.

"A tiny device was implanted inside her ear. Invisible to others, but it enables us to stay in touch with our spies," Admiral Zhala told him.

"Admiral, who is this?" a low female voice said suddenly.

Brenn had not heard her approach.

"This is General Brenn Mildash. Brenn, meet one of my most trusted spies, Elasha."

"General. I have heard many stories of your heroism. It is an honor to meet you," Elasha said.

"Come into the shadows," the admiral said.

Brenn was surprised at Elasha's appearance. She was very tall for a woman, almost as tall as he was. Raven-black hair was pulled back tightly from a handsome face. He thought it handsome because Elasha looked more male than female. "Evening, Elasha. I hope you will be able to help us. What do you know of the Toubosian ships hiding in Cewrick's courtyard? And do you have any knowledge of captured Ierilians?"

"I've learned much in the past week. There's been a lot of activity within the castle. The Toubosians have teamed up with Cewrick to gain control of our planet. From what I have heard, they are renegades. I believe their empress has no knowledge of their purpose."

Brenn fidgeted impatiently. "Prisoners? Ierilian captives? Do you have any knowledge about this?"

"Yes. They are being held in the dungeons in the deepest dungeons of Cewrick's castle. I have not been able to get close to them. But I do know where they are."

"Do you know why they took our people? Why they burned one village to the ground?" Brenn asked.

"Apparently, the destruction of the village was done against Cewrick's wishes. He was very angry and punished the captain of that ship by making him walk into the Forbidden Forest. Without the protection spell, he was dead in seconds. Cewrick appointed another to act as captain. The people were taken to obtain the secrets to the ore and crystals, how they can use it to create a weapon that could destroy the royal palace. Cewrick has been sending small groups of miners to work the mines. No one has talked, but they do work the mines, as they fear death by Cewrick's hand and his magick."

"Do the miners return to the castle at night?" Brenn asked.

"They work in shifts. One crew leaves, then they come back to the dungeons, and another crew is sent to the mines. Cewrick is determined to learn the secrets of the ore and the crystals."

"I'm surprised the Toubosian ships did not explode," Brenn said.

"Cewrick had a protective spell around them. The spell does not last long, but it was enough to keep the ships functioning. I cannot tell you much more than that. All of our people are alive. The children are kept in a separate area, away from the dungeons. They are treated well but are being brainwashed by Cewrick's so-called teachers. The babies and very young ones are cared for by some of Cewrick's women in a different section of the castle."

"How can we save our people? Do you have any thoughts on this?" Brenn asked.

"Yes, there is a way. But the disappearance of so many will invoke Cewrick's wrath. And there are always two groups that have been sent to work the mines. They're guarded by Toubosians."

"What is that way? Tell us," Brenn demanded. "All we want to do right now is rescue our people. We'll have to come up with a different plan to stop Cewrick and the renegade Toubosians. He will never learn the secrets of the ore and crystals, not from our people, but it sounds like he's determined to try and take over rulership of our planet, regardless."

"He's a powerful sorcerer. The disappearance of his captives will raise his ire and could cause a huge upheaval on our planet."

Admiral Zhala finally entered the conversation. "His ire be damned. So tell us how we can save our people."

"Tasar and I discovered a hidden entrance in the dungeons. I believe it is close to where our people are held. We came upon it by chance during midnight explorations. We saw a small metal handle, pulled it, and a large rock slid aside. Beyond is a maze of tunnels beneath the castle. We have not had time to map the complete tunnel system, but at least one of these tunnels leads to an entrance far beyond the Forbidden Forest. The entrance is located south of the forest in the foothills of the Turgor Mountains. We believe Cewrick has no knowledge of these tunnels."

Admiral Zhala frowned. "That seems odd. Cewrick has resided in that castle for centuries. The sorcerer has to be hundreds of years old."

"It is odd. I agree. Just inside the entrance is another metal handle that closes the entrance. It is barely visible to the naked eye. It is a miracle that Tasar spotted it when we were investigating."

"We could take the captured out through those tunnels, is that what you are telling us?" the admiral asked.

"Yes. But how do we release them from their captivity? They are guarded day and night, as are the children and the infants."

"We are not alone. But we will need more stealth ships to transport everyone. Brenn, let us return to the ship and report to the king. Elasha, you are relieved of duty. I am not sending you back in," Admiral Zhala ordered.

"No. I want to help, and you need Tasar and me. The other three spies do not know about the tunnels. Tasar and I kept it to ourselves."

"Elasha, I'm concerned that you have not reported any of this to me," the admiral told her.

"This has all happened recently, and I'm very seldom in a position to speak so you can hear me. Even at night, we are not alone. We sleep in huge chambers, at least twenty men and women to each chamber, sometimes more. If you could read my thoughts, it would help," Elasha remarked and grimaced. "Escaping from the sleep chambers at night to meet with Tasar was hard enough without getting caught, and I doubt our communication device would have worked inside the tunnels. We're too far below ground."

"First we need to free our people. After that, we will concentrate on the Toubosians and Cewrick and their plan to take over the planet. All right, Elasha, I suppose we do need you. We will need you to guide us through the tunnels when the time comes. General Mildash and I will return to the ship. When would be the best time to initiate this rescue?"

"Tonight. About five hours from now, most in the castle will be sleeping, and there will be minimal security. Many of them have a false sense of safety, thinking that nothing or no one can infiltrate Cewrick's castle. After they do a final check on all the prisoners, I heard gossip that they usually get drunk on eldalas spirit. It makes it easier for us to explore the castle at night. What about the other spies? Do you wish them to remain there?"

"Yes. We need to know what Cewrick and the Toubosians are planning at all times. I will contact you when to meet us so you and Tasar can lead us."

Elasha disappeared as fast as she had appeared. She had slunk into the shadows. Brenn and the admiral hurried back to the ship.

Once they were back inside and sat at the console, the admiral turned to Brenn. "What do you think?"

"How many can a stealth ship hold? We need to rescue them as fast as possible," Brenn said.

"Yes. I agree. But what about the miners?"

"We need to send a ship to each of the mines with space warriors aboard. They must not be afraid to kill. We need to get all of our people out of Cewrick's clutches. Now." Brenn clenched his jaw. If the admiral did not cooperate, he would call in his favors with the king and set up the rescue himself.

He need not have worried.

"Brenn, we need to plan this calmly. Rushing in would not be good. The rescue of the miners and those held in the castle must be coordinated. We need to plan accordingly. Contact the king. Tell him what Elasha has told us."

"I will. You inform our crew."

Brenn went to the private room and contacted Biryn. After Brenn had relayed everything, the king said, "I can confirm that Empress Khatari of Toubosia knew nothing of this plot. She informed me that the three ships were stolen by a renegade faction and her security team was unable to track them. The attack was not sanctioned by her or the Toubosian council. The empress was appalled. She offered her assistance, but I assured her that we are handling it. I will send enough stealth ships to transport our people and several more to rescue the miners. Good work, Brenn."

"Admiral Zhala and his spies deserve the praise. I have much more to tell you, but that can wait until after our return. How soon can we expect the ships? I am sending you the coordinates right now."

CHAPTER FOURTEEN

Ivran spoke up after Brenn climbed back into his chair behind the console. "What did you find out? You are keeping us in the dark, Brenn."

"Admiral Zhala and I will come up with a strategy to save our people. They are all alive and held in the dungeons of the castle."

"Dungeons? By the gods. My baby?"

"Ivran, from what I was told, the children and infants are well cared for. I have been in contact with the king. When the admiral and I have everything planned, we'll inform you. Stop fretting."

"You would be fretting, too, if your woman and child were in that castle and held by that villain."

"Yes, I do not doubt it. Be patient. Before this night has ended, you *will* see your mate and child." Brenn sighed.

"We will be landing close to Turgor in a few moments," Admiral Zhala said as he prepared the ship to land.

Brenn was seated in front of a digitized map of Ierilia and zoomed in to the Turgor foothills and Cewrick's realm. "There's not much time to plan this mission and relay the details to our rescue ships. Laro and Ivran will stand watch while we plan. I'm not as certain as your spy is that these tunnels are unknown to Cewrick."

Admiral Zhala joined him at the planning table after he landed the ship. "I trust Elasha's judgment in this. Her instincts have not led her astray yet."

Brenn gave Admiral Zhala a hard look. "I would rather prepare for the unexpected. We will plan this rescue with the expectation that the tunnels may have been compromised. We should be prepared for an ambush within the tunnel maze. Should our mission be compromised before we reach our people in the castle, the other teams will be authorized to rescue our people at the mines."

"Agreed. I believe our best course of action would be to infiltrate the castle through the tunnels with two small teams. Once we are inside the tunnel network, one team will split off with Elasha to rescue the adults, and the other team will go with Tasar to rescue the children. We can use stealth ships to safely drop warriors to rescue our people in the mines. We can transport the miners near Troncania, but I do not want to risk the ships close to the koriam crystal mines. The warriors will need to approach the mines on foot. After they've taken care of the guards, we'll have them lead our people to a safe zone for pickup."

"That's my assessment as well. We'll lead our people through the tunnels to the transport ships here. Once we have them safely into the tunnels, we can also arm some of the adults and task them to get the children to safety. We will guard their retreat from the tunnel maze and ensure the children are safe.

"I will make arrangements for their transport to the medical center after we get them aboard the stealth ships. Once everyone has been cleared medically, the king will ensure they have proper lodging until it is safe for them to return to their homes," the admiral said.

Brenn agreed and stood up from the table. "Admiral,

please contact the ships and relay our plan to them. I will update Laro and Ivran. I know they will want to be a part of the rescue team."

Brenn walked to the front of the ship where Ivran and Laro were keeping watch and explained the details of the mission. "I want you both on the rescue teams. We still have not determined who could have been filtering information to Cewrick, and I trust you to protect our people."

Ivran sighed in relief. "I was worried you would force me to stay with the ship, and I cannot do that knowing that Reana and Issa are trapped in that castle."

Brenn placed his hand on Ivran's shoulder and looked at his pain-filled face. "I would not dream of it, my friend."

"Your dragon circled above us earlier. How does she know where we will be? It is like she is always one step ahead of us," Laro said.

"I do not know how she knows, but I'm thankful for it," Brenn said as he glanced out at the sky, hoping to catch a glimpse of her. *I am thankful as well.* He smiled as Ciara's whisper touched his mind.

I have checked the area. It is safe here, and I will keep it so. You will not have to worry about your people on this side of the tunnels. There is an outcropping of rocks on the left side of the ship. I am there waiting for you.

"We have a couple of hours before we meet with Admiral Zhala's spies at the entrance of the tunnel. I will return momentarily. I must speak with Ciara before this mission starts," Brenn told them as he opened the hatch and walked down the steps of the ship to meet Ciara.

Brenn's breath caught in his throat at the sight of her hidden in the shadows of the outcropping. She was in human form, her long raven hair hanging down to her naked hips, her violet eyes meeting his as she ran into his open arms. She felt so small and fragile, it was hard to remember that she was a fierce predator in her own right, the beautiful dragon that had claimed him as hers.

"I cannot follow you when you enter the tunnels. I will not be able to protect you," Ciara said as she kissed him tenderly on the lips. *But allow me to give you this gift,* she whispered in his mind. She held him tightly as she deepened their kiss and a whisper of magick filled him.

Brenn's body ignited on fire as he sensed the soft tendrils of her magick sink into his skin and pierce him all the way to his split souls. The lion roared within him, desperate for freedom, fighting for dominance. The pain was so excruciating he thought he would be ripped asunder. Then intense pleasure filled him, so extreme, he was sure he would die from it. A connection was made, small, but just enough that it made the lion roar in triumph and the human gasp at the power that flowed through his veins. Slowly the tendrils pulled away from his body, Ciara's whispers quieting in his mind.

Brenn opened his eyes to gaze at his beautiful lifemate. He was not sure what she had done to him, but he could *feel* her. Their connection had grown stronger in a matter of minutes, but she had also given him a connection to his lion. He felt the predator united with him instead of fighting for freedom. The power of the lion, its quick reflexes, incredible speed, and heightened senses were now his in his human form, and he felt invigorated by it.

"I was not sure if I would succeed. By the goddess, it worked!" Ciara whispered excitedly.

"But how? Can you do this for Ivran and Laro?"

"Oh, my love, I am so sorry, but there's nothing I can do for your friends. I was grasping at straws to try this spell. My magick is so limited. I only succeeded because we are lifemates, but you still cannot shift, because you would still lose your humanity. I cannot break the curse. I could only give you a connection to your lion because your soul is tied to mine."

Brenn hugged her close, kissing the top of her head, enjoying the feel of her in his arms. "Thank you for this gift, my beautiful enchantress."

Ciara pulled back and looked up at him. He noticed the serious expression in her eyes. "Save your people, Brenn. Do not let Cewrick determine their fate. Save them as I could not save mine."

"When we defeat Cewrick, and I say when, not if, will the curse not be lifted from your people? Will not the black dragons change back and once again grace the skies with their jewel beauty as told in our legends?"

She did not answer. Brenn stepped back helplessly as her body shimmered and her scales grew, indicating the start of her shift back to that of the dragon. When the purple dragon turned her head to look at him, he reached up to brush the scales along her neck. "We will break all his curses, Ciara. We will defeat Cewrick and find a way to free all of us."

Ciara nudged him with her nose, pushing him back toward the ship. *Go, my love. Your people await their rescue.*

Brenn walked back and boarded the ship to be met by the curious stares of Laro and Ivran. He wondered how much they could have seen from that distance. Gazing through the view window, he could see everything clearly, including the dragon hiding in the shadows.

"Strange, I could have sworn I briefly saw a beautiful naked woman," Ivran murmured.

"Hallucinations, my friend," Brenn said. He chuckled, but inwardly he knew he and Ciara had to be more careful.

CHAPTER FIFTEEN

Brenn set course for the Turgor Mountains. It only took minutes to arrive. He set the ship down below a ridge, close to the coordinates of the tunnel entrance where Elasha and Tasar would be waiting for them. The extra stealth ships had arrived. The admiral quickly brought the small contingents up to speed and ordered the pilots to stay with the ships.

As Brenn left the ship, he noticed the admiral behind him. "Admiral, the king would not want you along for this rescue. It is far too dangerous. He would never forgive me were anything to happen to you. You have not seen ground combat in how many years?"

Admiral Zhala opened his mouth to argue.

Brenn did not give him the chance to speak. "I am sorry, Admiral. If this were a space fight, I might have agreed. I know you outrank me in space battle, but I'm afraid I outrank you on the ground."

Admiral Zhala nodded, heaved a sigh, and reluctantly agreed to stay with the ship. "Be safe."

With Brenn leading, they made their way to the entrance,

darting from tree to tree, hiding in the shadows of the mountains. Though Ciara had told him all was safe, with Cewrick's strong magick, who knew what invisible danger could be lurking? Brenn constantly gazed up, looking for black dragons and urcals. Even with his lion's strength, he knew he could not best an urcal. Their claws could scoop up three or four humans in one swoop.

He hoped they were far enough away from the Sucronian Ridge and the castle and that the dragons and birds did not venture this far out.

"Pssst."

Brenn reached for his gun.

"Pssst, over here."

The whisper came from an outcrop of rocks. Brenn saw no entrance, no opening of any kind except a small gap at the bottom of the outcrop, just high enough for someone to lie down and roll beneath it. He held his hand up, indicating the others to stop.

"It is me. Lie down and roll beneath the rocks."

He recognized Elasha's voice once she spoke a little louder. He felt claustrophobic as he slid beneath the rock. It was inky black after the bright moonlight. Even after his eyes became accustomed to the darkness, he could see nothing. Shivers ran down his spine at the thought of kurakeldas, giant spiders that nested in the mountains. They were at least the size of an infant with huge, bulging red eyes and very hairy legs. Their bite was not lethal but could cause much damage to a human.

Dim light met him as he rolled into the tunnel. He stood and faced Elasha. While brushing sprigs and dirt off his hair, face, and clothes, he said, "And how do you propose to get the children through there?"

"The children will think it a game. The infants we'll need to tie to the adults with blankets, and they'll have to slide through on their backs."

One by one the others appeared.

Ivran spoke as soon as he made it through, as he wiped spider webs from his face. "Brenn, you could have warned us!"

Brenn shook his head at Ivran, then turned back to Elasha. "Where is Tasar?"

"Waiting for us near the end of the tunnel. It is a long way to the castle, and the tunnels are all very dark. I hope you brought glimmer sticks," Elasha said.

Brenn produced several from his belt. "I came prepared, as I'm sure the others did." He flicked a stick. Instantly, it lit up a good section of the tunnel. He handed one to Elasha. "Lead on. There's no time to waste."

Laro joined them. "Elasha, have you and Tasar checked the tunnels to make sure it is safe?"

"Without glimmer sticks or torches, it was hard. Usually, we grab a torch, but one of the guards woke up, so we had to do without. It is good we know the route so well. We did not hear anything on our way to the entrance. Tasar is waiting for us."

"And you have never seen any creatures lurking down here?" Brenn asked.

"Some kurakeldas and a few argali snakes. Nothing else. Tasar, you there?" Elasha called out.

Brenn heard an answering whistle. "When we get to the entrance of the dungeons, Tasar will lead all of you to rescue the children and the infants. Elasha and I will take care of the adults. Be careful. The young ones are not in the dungeons. They are in the castle but, from what Elasha has told us, well away from Cewrick's quarters. You may meet with resistance. Do not hesitate. Set your guns to kill."

"Even the women caring for the infants?" one of the space warriors asked.

"They are Cewrick's women. There's no humanity left in

them, if they are even females. Who knows if he used his magick to change some of his creatures into humanoids to care for the babies. Elasha, have you seen these women?" Brenn asked.

"Yes. They are strange-looking individuals."

"There you go. Do not hesitate. If even one woman or guard sets off the alarm, we are all done for. Now go. We'll meet you back here," Brenn told them.

Brenn and Elasha moved swiftly, but it seemed to take forever to traverse the tunnels. "We're here," Elasha finally said while reaching for a metal handle. "Be ready."

He took his weapon out of its holster and set it to kill. He hoped Elasha was right in that the guards would be drunk and passed out. Straightening his glimmer stick, he stuck it into his belt. A huge boulder slid open, revealing a space just big enough for a person. Elasha carefully stepped through. She motioned him to follow.

After rounding a bend, Elasha stopped. "There are three guards. Two are passed out. The third is still drinking."

Brenn looked over her shoulder. The trio did not look human, though they had the bodies of men, their hands were like claws and very large, with only four digits on each hand. Their heads were too big for their bodies and looked reptilian. "Handsome fellows. I bet you have had fun with them," Brenn said softly.

"Oh yeah. Getting kissed by one of them is really a turn on," Elasha hissed and sent him a dirty look.

"Sorry, I was joking. Time to incinerate them," he whispered. He first aimed at the one that was still drinking. In seconds, the creature was gone, turned into a small pile of white ashes. Brenn felt no remorse in taking care of the other two. "That was almost too easy," he muttered, then looked at the barred dungeons.

Scanning the people lying on the ground on dirty straw, he

spotted his father. "Father, wake up," he called out, hoping it was loud enough.

Not only did his father sit up, but several others did, too. "Brenn. By the gods. I knew we could count on you, son!"

"Hush. We do not want to raise alarms. Everything echoes in these caves."

Elasha said, "Nice of you to incinerate the keys, too."

"No problem. Stand back," he told the people, who were now all thronging near the bars. He quickly aimed his weapon at the lock, and it fell to the ground. He handed his weapon to Elasha. "Go and free the women. Make haste."

"Father, how many were sent to the mines to work?" Brenn asked as he began ushering everyone down the tunnel to the entrance.

"Usually groups of ten men and ten women."

A large group of women joined them. Brenn scanned their faces but did not see his mother among them. Maybe she had been sent to the mines. "The rescue of our people that were sent to the mines should be happening as we speak," Brenn told his father. "We need to travel fast. The young and strong need to assist some of our older people. The faster we get out of here, the better. Father, follow Elasha and take the lead. I will bring up the rear."

Yartah nodded. "Everyone, you need to stop talking and remain very quiet. All our lives depend on no alarms going off in the castle. If Cewrick gets wind of this escape, his wrath will hold no boundary. We also need to make haste. All of you young ones, assist your elderly grandparents."

Brenn chimed in. "The exit is quite far. Father, here is a glimmer stick."

Elasha led the way through the entrance. Brenn stood at the rear of the large group and constantly glanced behind to see if any other guards came from the other side or if there was any sign of Tasar and the crew, the children and infants.

He wondered what to do. Should he wait for them? Close the entrance, or leave it open? Getting all the people through the narrow opening had taken far too long. Tasar should have been back.

He hesitated, then was about to step through the opening, when he heard a sound. He stepped back, weapon ready, when he saw Tasar appear carrying two infants. Ivran followed close behind, a baby in each arm. All the warriors and adolescents carried small children. Brenn sighed in relief when he saw his sister Shanina among them. The group of children that could walk fast enough on their own all milled around him. Some looked awed as they gazed at Brenn.

Tasar looked tired. "That was no fun. I will tell you the tale later. Now, we must hurry. We killed near all the guards and women, but one managed to get away. The whole castle will be in an uproar by now."

"Great. Okay, children, follow Tasar and begin running through the tunnel as fast as you can. Here, give me one of those," Brenn offered and held his arm out for one of the infants Tasar carried.

The children were able to move much faster than the adults. Many of them were small enough to fit through the opening two at a time. It was difficult to hush them. Their young voices were crystal clear, echoing through the dungeons. Laro appeared last, also carrying an infant.

Brenn sent his friend a grin and motioned him on, then slipped through the opening himself and pulled the lever. The boulder slipped back into place. "That's one hurdle out of the way. Now to get to the other side as fast as we can. I know Elasha told us she did not think Cewrick knows of the tunnel network, but we cannot be sure."

The children moved so much faster that they caught up to the other group fast, the women quickly gathering their infants and children, relieving the men of their burdens.

Brenn watched Ivran embrace his mate and smiled. Ivran's choice had been hard — go with Brenn to save his mate or go with Tasar to rescue his baby.

They had traveled the tunnel for what seemed a very long time when suddenly there was a scream from one of the women. The group stopped. Brenn hurried to find out what had happened and saw a kurakelda munching on a woman's leg. It was Meena. He fired on the beast's large body and incinerated it. But the poor woman had several chunks missing from her leg and bled profusely. This could draw more of the creatures.

"Take your tunic off!" he yelled at one of the men. Using his knife, he quickly tore strips off it, and after binding the woman's leg at the thigh, he wrapped the other strips around the wounds. He helped her up, then aimed his weapon at the blood pooled on the granite rock. It was gone, but not fast enough to keep from attracting more of the spiders. Women screamed — children screamed and cried. He had to kill several of the hairy beasts before they receded into the crevices of the rock walls.

"Here, Meena, I will carry you the rest of the way. It should not be too far now." There was no way Meena would be able to walk, to put any weight on her injured leg. He knew her well. She was a distant cousin. How she was going to manage to roll beneath the outcrop, he had no idea. She was in a lot of pain.

He picked her up easily. As they continued on, one of the space warriors joined him. "General, I have some medical supplies. Something that will ease her pain."

"Thank you. That will help," Brenn said.

"My name is Domo Kecsi. I'm a medic, and I am so honored to be part of this mission." He dug in the pouch attached to his belt and brought out a small vial. He held it near Meena's lips and waited until she had swallowed all of it. "Once we are out of here, I have other medical supplies on our ship."

"Will this ease her pain enough for her to roll beneath the rock?" Brenn asked.

"Yes, it should last a while. It is quite powerful. We will need to wrap her leg better, though. If dirt gets into those wounds, it could cause a serious infection," Domo warned.

"When we get to the exit, I will ask for another tunic we can tear into strips."

Brenn estimated it had to be near sunup when they finally got to the exit without further incidents, except for the babies and very young infants crying and getting restless. Moving everyone through the narrow gap was going to take a long time and be quite a chore. He decided the children and youngest people should go first, then the older people assisted by a younger person. After that, the women with infants. But first, Meena should go, assisted by Domo. She needed care, and fast.

Once Meena and Domo had advanced far enough, the children began to roll through, two at a time. They regarded it somewhat like a game. Brenn grimaced. At such a young age, he would have thought it a game, too. He wondered if any of them would remember the seriousness of the whole situation, or if they would remember it as the adventure of their lives.

The women with infants tightly bound to their chests were next. They could not roll—they had to shuffle their way out on their backs, which took a lot longer, of course.

When Brenn finally rolled out of the exit, the suns had risen in full. *I am so glad you are safe, my love.* He glanced up at the sky and held his hand above his eyes. Very high up, he saw a speck and knew it was Ciara. *If you look at that tall aegrolia tree, at the base of its trunk grows a large purple flower. Get that flower. Crush its petals and place it on the wounded woman's bites. It will heal her.*

"How do I explain that? And how did you even know about it?" he murmured.

Though I could not communicate with you while you were inside the tunnels and castle, I knew everything that was happening. Explain to the medic that it is an old cure that your grandmother taught you.

"Okay. I think…" Brenn responded. Her voice in his mind was like nectar. He hurried to the base of the tree and saw the lone purple flower. He quickly picked it and brought it to Domo.

Domo looked at him curiously. "A flower?"

"Do not ask too many questions. Crush the petals of this flower and place the paste on Meena's wounds. It will heal her. My grandmother taught me this a long time ago, but the flower is extremely rare," Brenn told him.

Domo looked a bit doubtful. "I suppose it cannot hurt."

"Do it. That is an order," Brenn said sternly.

Brenn's father joined him and finally embraced his son. "Thank you, son. Your mother is not with our group. She must have been taken to the mines. You will notify me when she is safe? We will talk later. The ships are waiting, I was told, though we cannot see them."

"You will all be taken to the medical facility first. After that, you, Mother, Shanina, Laro and his son, and Ivran and his family will all live with me on my estate until our village has been rebuilt." He saw his father's raised eyebrows. Right, they did not know the village had been burned to the ground. He would tell them later. He continued, "Until all danger from Cewrick has passed, and that bastard has been annihilated, this is how it has to be. I will see you all soon, Father."

CHAPTER SIXTEEN

The rescue at the mines had not gone off without a hitch. Two space warriors had lost their lives fighting the guards. It was always a sad time when warriors gave up their lives to fight for their king. But Brenn, though he felt sad for the warriors' families, could not help but feel joyful at the safe return of all his people.

Waiting in his home for his family and friends, he felt impatient, wanting to speed up the medical examinations, but of course, that was not an option. His respite would be brief. There was still the biggest mission—to finally get rid of Cewrick, once and for all. The sorcerer had rained havoc on their planet long enough, and his latest stunt had beaten everything.

Brenn relaxed on the porch that overlooked his estate, a goblet of wine at his lips. He had just barely arrived home, bathed, and finally relaxed, clothed in a soft robe. And there she was, hovering in the sky, high enough that people would think she was merely a bird. "I long for you, my love," he whispered. He knew she could not change into her human until after the suns disappeared over the horizon.

And I for you. I will come to you after the suns set and you go to your sleeping quarters. I am jealous of the woman that bathes you.

She has no right to touch my man.

"Jealous?" Brenn asked softly. "Silly. She is just a bathing servant."

She has pleasured you.

"Not anymore. She merely washes my back and my hair. There is only one for me now. My beautiful dragon lady."

His communicator interrupted his conversation with Ciara. It was Domo. "What can I do for you?"

"General, I apologize for disturbing you. Can you give me the name of the flower you gave me?"

"Domo, I do not know. My grandmother has gone to the field of dreams, so I cannot ask her. I only knew what it looked like."

"It is a miracle flower. After I crushed the petals and mixed them with some sterile water, I placed the mixture on Meena's wounds. They healed very fast, and she has no blemishes on her legs. Do you realize what this flower could do for medical science? For our warriors that are hurt when fighting?" Domo asked.

"I'm so sorry. I cannot help you."

"I have never seen a flower like it. I took an image of it before I crushed the petals and researched it, but I cannot find it anywhere in our databases."

"It is a rare flower. My grandmother told me there are very few. It was a stroke of luck that one happened to be growing near the entrance and I saw it. I'm so glad that Meena healed well."

Domo sounded very disappointed when he answered. "If you can ever remember the name of the flower, can you contact me?"

"I sure will," Brenn promised. He knew it was Ciara's magick, but no way could he divulge that to Domo. Maybe one day in the future when Cewrick had been defeated, her magick could help everyone. For now, it had to remain a secret. *She* had to remain a secret.

The time passed too slowly. He returned to his room and dressed in a comfortable red tunic and black pants. He was so anxious for his family to arrive, but he knew so many families were separated for now. It was a long, drawn-out process to reunite parents with their children, then assign them to temporary living quarters until they could return to their homes. But there was one family that would still be missing a baby. They needed to locate little Shuri's parents.

Brenn picked up the communicator and contacted Domo. "Domo, I need you to locate a Troncanian family among the adults we rescued. They will have or will be reporting that their infant was left behind in their home when they were abducted. They will more than likely fear that the baby did not survive. My two friends and I found her. She was placed with a family on the outskirts of the city. You can reassure the parents that the infant is alive and healthy."

"I am sure that baby is here in the medical center. I was with the team that answered a call to pick up an abandoned Troncanian infant a few days ago. A beautiful baby with a head full of copper curls."

"That must be her. I'm relieved to hear she was taken to the medical center."

"I will make sure she is reunited with her family."

"Thank you," Brenn said and closed the communicator. He knew Ivran and Laro would be as relieved as he was to know little Shuri would be returned to her family.

The sound of running footsteps sounded behind him.

"Brenn!" his sister, Shanina, exclaimed.

He turned and captured her in a hug and saw that his parents along with Ivran and his mate followed close behind her. Ivran carried his daughter in his arms.

"I'm so glad you are safe and unhurt," Brenn said as he hugged his mother. "I was so worried when you were not with the group my team rescued."

When his mother looked up at him, her eyes and cheeks were wet with tears. "I knew nothing would stop you from finding us. Is it true about our home? We overheard talk at the medical center. Is Xynnar really destroyed?"

Brenn wiped the tears from her cheek and held her close. "Do not cry, Mother. It is all true. When the Toubosians kidnapped all of you, they destroyed everything. Do not think of that now. You are here, and you are safe."

"Brenn...did you know there is a purple dragon sleeping in your courtyard?" Shanina asked while pointing to the courtyard with an expression of wonder on her face.

"Yes, little sister, I do know, but you must keep her a secret. You cannot tell anyone about her," he warned her as he ruffled her hair. Shanina was barely sixteen and had always been fascinated by the legends of the jeweled dragons. "Laro will return tomorrow with Tomas and Twink."

Shanina gasped in surprise. "I was so worried about him! When the ship came, and the Toubosians captured us, they frightened him, and he ran off. How did you find him?"

Brenn smiled down at Shanina. "He surprised me when he tackled me by the stream the night I found Ivran. We left him with Tomas in Arluc. Come, I know all of you must be hungry and weary from your ordeal. I will meet you in the dining room when you have had a chance to bathe. My staff has laid out fresh clothing for you all." Brenn led the group from the porch to the hall where one of his staff was waiting to show them to their rooms.

As his family left to freshen up, Brenn walked back out to the porch and rested his hands on the railing. Looking out over the courtyard, he spotted his beautiful lifemate. "I'm relieved to have my family safe, but I find myself impatient to hold you in my arms. Is it wrong to feel this way?"

I am impatient as well, my love. Go. Enjoy your meal with your family. Revel in their safe return. I will be with you when the moons arise.

Brenn joined his family in the private dining room of his suite as the suns were setting. Ivran and his mate chose to have dinner sent to their suite, not wanting to leave their sleeping baby with a staff member. He understood Ivran's need to stay close to Issa and his mate. Brenn would do the same if the tables were turned. They ate a light meal of makulel, jago cheese, and a variety of fruits and vegetables laid out as a buffet by the staff. During dinner they discussed menial things, all of them avoiding the discussion of what had happened to their homes.

Brenn could see how weary his parents really were, and Shanina had drifted off to sleep leaning against his side. He quietly carried his sister to her room as his parents retired to their own.

He laid his sister gently on the bed and brushed the hair away from her face. "Sleep well, little sister," he said as he bent down and kissed her forehead.

Brenn left his sister and returned to his suite to stroll out onto the balcony. The moons rose heavy in the sky, their light shining on the courtyard below him, but there was no sign of Ciara. He gazed up at the sky, hoping to catch a glimpse of those scales flashing as she glided by, but there was still no sign of her. He knew she had to be close. Because of her gift, he could sense her presence.

Perplexed, he strode back into his suite and noticed a faint glow radiating from his bathing chamber. His breath caught as he peered into the chamber and saw her. Her delicate scales flashed in the soft light, droplets of water glittering like fire opals, leaving wet shining trails on her beautiful alabaster skin. She was exquisite. If the king's minstrel could see her, he would write songs about her almost ethereal beauty.

He hurriedly removed his clothing and walked to the sunken baths. Standing on the first step, he was mesmerized by the glow in the water--a myriad of swirling rainbow colors, and the scent of axania bells, a tiny flower that grew in abundance on Ierilia, drifted to his nostrils.

"What kind of magick produces rainbow bathing waters," he murmured and gazed into her beckoning eyes.

"The magick of love," Ciara said softly.

Lost in the depth of her gaze, he walked down the steps into the water and approached her. She spread her legs, and he lowered his body into the water. With both hands on the edge of the marble tiles, he sought her lips. They parted, and her tongue entered his mouth, danced with his, explored every crevice of his mouth. When she sucked his tongue, he groaned. His cock was hard as a tree trunk, his sack taut and aching. He pulled away from her lips and kissed her nose, her forehead, her chin. His fingers stroked every detail of her face as if painting her into his mind.

"Wash me, my love. Then let us retire to your bed," she murmured.

Brenn's heart thundered in his ears, hammered in his chest, blood surging through his veins, to his cock, causing him to almost erupt. How could he hold out for that long? "Wench, you torture me," he told her, but he reached for a flask. Taking the stopper off, he poured the liquid into both palms of his hands, then began to wash her. Starting from the base of her neck, he slowly massaged her shoulders, then slid his hands to her breasts, stopping long enough to tease her nipples to sharp little points. Gods, she was beautiful. Those enticing scales of hers glistened with the rainbow colors of the water, her body arching to meet his questing hands as he continued his exploration.

When he came to her downy mound, her swollen lips, her hips lifting to meet his hand, it was too much. Such pleasurable heat seared his skin, shooting straight to his cock, he could not stop his semen from bursting loose. He groaned and bit his lip as his cock spasmed in release. It was obvious what had happened, and her tinkling laughter aroused his passion again.

"That will make our joining so much sweeter," Ciara said sweetly. "You had too much pent-up passion that would have exploded upon entering me."

He continued his teasing exploration between her folds, gently entering a finger into her pulsing, moist vagina, his thumb on her clit. She gasped in pleasure as his thumb circled her sensitive little nub. "Finish washing me, my warrior, and I will service you," she murmured.

Removing his finger from her swollen flesh, he quickly washed her legs, her feet, and each dainty toe, then lay beside her in the huge bath.

Ciara moved to straddle his legs, took the flask, and poured a liberal amount into her hands. Her breathing was heavy as she washed him. She took her time, her hands gliding across his heated body, exploring his chest, the hard ridges of his abdomen, then teasingly trailing to his cock. It had already sprung back to life, his sack taut again, but without the fierce ache. He moaned as her fingers wrapped around his girth and slowly pumped up and down the length of him. Loosening her grip, she slowly slid her hand back up his body, scorching his skin along its path.

"We are ready, my love." Ciara stood and held out her hand.

Brenn allowed her to lead him out of the baths. They stopped long enough to quickly dry. Then she led him up the steps and into his bedchamber. The staff had made his bed with fresh linens, but surely they had not done this? The covers were pulled back, and he looked at a bed of crimson ambrosia petals. "You have been busy," he murmured as she fell back onto the bed, pulling him down on top of her.

He took her into his arms and pulled her up against the pillows. He gazed into her passion-dark eyes, "I love you, my dragon siren. I wish this night would not end."

Ciara placed her finger against his lips. "Ssh. Our day will come. Let us enjoy our pleasure this night without thought of the future. If you can just hold me in your arms, we can pretend everything around us will disappear."

"Alas, the future is always there," he replied. He kissed her lips, then trailed down to her glimmering scales. He licked them. They felt so smooth, so fragile. Taking a nipple into his mouth, he sucked hard and could swear he tasted nectar in his mouth. Was that even possible? Reaching down, he pushed a finger all the way inside her, rotating it, until he felt the walls of her center relax, then entered another finger, stretching her further.

Her hand had reached down, her fingers encasing his cock. She pulled the skin back and forth, her hand sliding from base to tip, causing him to moan in pleasure.

He spread her legs wide, then sat on his knees between them and drank in the beauty of her spread lips, the rosy clitoris throbbing invitingly, her tight sheath beckoning, pearly liquid oozing down between her slit. He lifted her feet and placed her legs over his shoulders, his cock inching toward her opening.

Leaning forward, he grasped her breasts, kneading, tweaking her nipples, as he entered her with one thrust, filling her completely. She gasped and bucked her hips up against him.

"Yes, my love, oh yes. More, please…more," she begged.

He did not need to be told again and began to pump within her.

"Harder, my love, harder! I'm not made of glass."

Brenn drove into her as hard as he could, then fell atop her and took her into his arms. Burying his face in her mane of fragrant, still-wet hair, he could feel his climax approaching.

When Ciara wrapped her legs around him and met his

thrusts, he shuddered, his release imminent.

"Yes, oh yes, my love," Ciara shouted as he felt her sheath tighten and spasm around his cock with her own release.

They lay quietly for a while until their breathing calmed. Brenn rolled off her and lay beside her. He leaned on his elbow and gazed down at her. "Ciara, my love, there is so much I do not know about you. Do you have parents? Did they fall under Cewrick's curse?"

"Yes, they did, and are now black dragons."

"Was your father a sorcerer, or your mother a sorceress? Were you born with your gift? How many sorcerers and sorceresses are there on Ierilia? Did all the jewel dragons have the gift of magick?" he asked.

"So many questions all at once. No, only one has the gift. My father is the king of my clan. He had lived for more than a thousand years when I came of age. When a sorcerer's or sorceress' offspring come of age, the gift of magick is transferred to him or her, and the parent becomes the teacher," she told him.

"And the parent loses his or her magick completely?"

Ciara shook her head. "No, not completely, but their offspring's magick is much more powerful. If the curse is ever lifted, my magick will be more powerful than Cewrick's."

"Then how was it possible for Cewrick to place the curse on your people? Could you not have defeated him?" Brenn needed to know.

"Cewrick came like a thief in the night, much like he did with Xynnar. The curse was upon us before we knew what was happening. Oh, Brenn, I wish you could have seen our jewel mountains, our valley, before Cewrick wreaked his havoc. It was a paradise. I know no human can ever set foot in those mountains. The cliffs are impossible to scale, but if the curse is ever lifted, I can fly you there on my dragon," she said softly.

"You are a princess, then, and will one day be a queen?"

"I suppose. Does that change the way you feel?"

"By the gods, no. You are my lifemate. We are bound for all eternity," he said in a grumbling tone. "How would your parents feel about us?"

"I do not know. A mating between a human, even less a lion shifter, has never occurred in all our history."

"My sweet princess, I hate to ask, but do you think your parents survived?"

"I know they did. I saw them change into black dragons. But the black dragons have no memory of anything. They do Cewrick's bidding."

A tear trickled down her cheek, and he bent to lick it away. "I am sorry. We should speak of happier things, like today's rescue."

She laughed softly. "And I am ready for more of you, my warrior."

Brenn's communicator went off. He really did not want to answer it, but under the circumstances, he had no choice. Annoyed at the interruption, he picked it up and stabbed at the button.

"This is Admiral Zhala. I have interesting news from one of my spies."

"Like?"

"It seems Cewrick took a fancy to Alyndra. She is a very pretty female spy. He invited her to his private quarters, of course attempted to seduce her, but he was very drunk. She managed to get him talking."

Brenn sighed. "Do not stop now and keep me in suspense."

"Cewrick apparently fathered a child, a son. When the son came of age, his magick was greater than Cewrick's. The boy's mother was favored by the Goddess Rania, the goddess of all sorcery. When the baby was born, Rania blessed him."

"Where is the son now? This is the first I have ever heard

of Cewrick having an offspring," Brenn said.

"When Cewrick found out about the boy's future powers and strength, he killed the woman. Then he placed a curse on his son and banished him to the bowels of Ierilia. He lives there in caves and tunnels as some kind of monster worm."

"And you find this interesting? I find it inhuman," Brenn told the admiral.

"Patience. It appears the son is the only one able to defeat his father, if he were to be released from his prison and the curse lifted."

"Do not even think it. No one knows how to get to the bowels of Ierilia."

"The entrance lies below the dungeons and tunnel network we were in."

"I will speak to the king, but it is far too dangerous a mission. Even if we managed to go down to the bowels and we found the worm, then what? The thought of such a mission is unfeasible and beyond our capabilities."

"Cewrick is beyond furious, Alyndra told me. He has already taken his anger out on many of his followers. His rage roars throughout the castle."

"I expected as much," Brenn answered.

"Wait, what's that I hear?" the admiral said.

The communicator crackled. The transmission was lost. Brenn looked at Ciara, who sat up, her scales beginning to grow.

"I must leave, my warrior. I will contact you soon," she said. She slipped off the bed and hurried out to the verandah.

Brenn could barely see her anymore. The moons were shadowed by black clouds that were getting thicker and thicker. He had hurried after her to see her change. Then she flew away, high up. All moonlight disappeared. In the distance, he saw a strange phenomenon. A black funnel swirled toward his home. It ripped out trees and everything in its path. He had never seen anything like it. He was about to go warn his guests and the staff when he noticed Ciara.

She breathed no fire, but a blueish streak issued from her mouth aimed directly at the funnel. It stopped, changed direction, then slowly disintegrated. Then she breathed up at the black clouds, and soon, the sky was clear of them, and only the stars and moons were visible.

I have to go, Brenn. There are more of these all over Ierilia. Be careful. Cewrick is out for revenge.

Brenn hurried back to his bed, retrieved the communicator, and hailed the admiral. "The threat is gone. At least from our city."

He was still speaking to the admiral when he heard Ciara give him more news.

Brenn, Cewrick has turned people to stone statues in quite a few villages all over our planet. There is nothing I can do to stop this. My magick is not strong enough.

Brenn relayed the information to the admiral. "I just heard. By the gods, that monster is turning many of our people into stone statues."

"What can we do?" Zhala asked.

"Nothing right now. We will meet tomorrow."

It was not long before he heard the flapping of Ciara's wings. He ran to his balcony and saw her in the courtyard. Her beautiful purple eyes gazed up at him. He saw large tears drip to the ground, flowers sprouting where the tears had seeped in between the flagstones.

I am so sorry, my love, I stopped the black storm and the funnels, but I could not contain the statue curse. Cewrick has halted his sorcery for now, as the suns are about to rise. We are facing so much more. This is not how I wanted our night to end.

"No, but we have the memory to feed on. We will defeat Cewrick, and all curses will be lifted." His steady gaze held hers. "I love you, my dragon princess. You are the song that sings in my soul."

And I love you, my warrior prince. Go and rest while you can, for tomorrow we face yet another mountain, but we will stand on it and be victorious.

WATCH FOR CRIMSON REALM BOOK 2
THE DRAGON'S LION

The rescue of Brenn's pride sets off an angry tirade from Cewrick that results in curses that almost cripple the Crimson Realm and all of Ierilia.

With the help of Ciara, Brenn leads his crew through the bowels of the planet and the Forbidden Forest to unlock the secret of defeating Cewrick. But will his defeat end the reign of terror on their world?

EXCERPT

The king quickly stepped toward Brenn and hugged him. "It is good to see you, my friend. The rescue went well."

"Yes, but now we face Cewrick's wrath, as you have witnessed," Brenn answered, disengaging from the hug.

Biryn filled three goblets with wine. "Aldis should be here any moment," he told Brenn.

He had no sooner spoken, and the admiral arrived. "Aldis, congratulations on a successful mission," the king exclaimed, holding out a goblet.

"The praise goes to Brenn and his men. He told me to stay with the ship," the admiral grumbled.

"And for good reason, I presume?" The king looked at

Brenn.

"The admiral is not used to ground missions or combat. I did not want to risk his life," Brenn told Biryn.

"Good decision. But now we face the wrath of the sorcerer. Cewrick has unleashed his minions upon us. Aldis, why did not you annihilate the swarm of black dragons and urcals?"

"Brenn told me that many of the black dragons were once jewel dragons or humans. When the curse is lifted, they will return to their former state. Since the urcals and dragons flew as a flock, I could not attack," Aldis explained.

"I would not see the jewel dragons harmed or any humans. I abide by the decision, but many of Ierilia's people were abducted before the warning transmission went out. What do you suggest we do in case of another attack?" the king asked.

"Cewrick's attacks can come in many forms. He has spies among us. He could use his magick and create other spells, or he could use his black dragons and urcals to attack again," Brenn said.

"What about your jewel dragon? Can she not help?" the king wondered.

"No, not against a swarm of them. She is but one and feeling helpless right now. It took a lot of her energy to fight the black wind funnels. She could not undo the stone curse. Her magick cannot come into full force until Cewrick is slain. And there is only one that can help us annihilate him," Brenn said.

"Who?"

"His son."

"Cewrick has a son? That is news to me," Biryn said, his face a picture of incredulity.

NEXT IN THE CRIMSON REALM CHRONICLES

The Dragon's Lion

Sword of Betrayal

Sword of Judgement

OTHER BOOKS COMING SOON IN THIS SERIES:

Testing the Crown – Book 5

Shard in the Mirror – Book 6

Initiation Genesis – Book 7

Tabeka's Revenge – Book 8

Danger, lies, and betrayal forge the path to unlocking the secrets Brenn seeks.

The Dragon's Lion

Crimson Realm Chronicles 2

TARYN JAMESON **GABRIELLA BRADLEY**

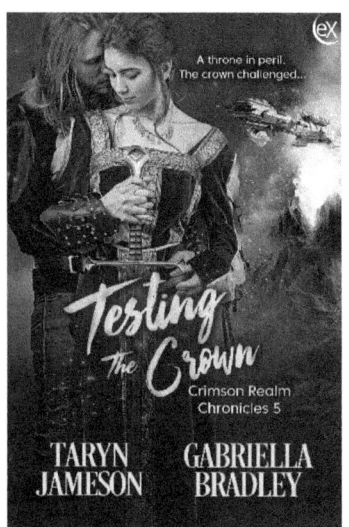

A throne in peril. The crown challenged...

Testing The Crown

Crimson Realm Chronicles 5

TARYN JAMESON **GABRIELLA BRADLEY**

The blade of betrayal cuts deep.

Sword Of Betrayal

Crimson Realm Chronicles 3

TARYN JAMESON **GABRIELLA BRADLEY**

The blade of justice is a double-edged sword.

Sword Of Judgement

Crimson Realm Chronicles 4

TARYN JAMESON **GABRIELLA BRADLEY**

ABOUT THE AUTHORS

Taryn Jameson

Taryn Jameson is a mother, artist, and avid reader who lives in an enchanted forest that sparks her imagination to create. Her latest outlet is the written word. She is the alter ego of cover artist Angela Waters.

Gabriella Bradley

Gabriella Bradley has been a writer and artist all her. Her hobbies include hiking, gardening, swimming, sewing, embroidery. Favorite movies are old timers like Gone with the Wind, Spartacus etc. Favorite music is Abba.

www.ingramcontent.com/pod-product-compliance
Lightning Source LLC
Chambersburg PA
CBHW071254130626
46556CB00003B/1311